Memoirs
of a
Female Messiah

CINDY LEE BERRYHILL

Memoirs
of a
Female Messiah

The Story of Me, Michelle Domingue

A Novel

Entwhistle Books

Cover photo by Greg Allen
Book design by Jeff Schalles

The author would like to thank: Tami Berryhill, Lois Navrkal, Lynne Robinson, Paul Harrington, Morgan Entrekin, my fifth grade teacher in Oroville CA Mr. Hutchins, and especially Paul Williams, all of whom encouraged my writing of this book in different and important ways.

ISBN 0-934558-24-8

First printing

published by:
Entwhistle Books
Box 232517
Encinitas CA 92023 USA

Cindy Lee Berryhill Tearaway Page:
www.mwpsoft.com/clb/

Foreword

— by Mr. Apricot
(excerpted from *In and Out of Bed with
Michelle Domingue*)

Oh my Michelle
    This is a song for you
My Mia Michelle
    Domingue oh my loved one
Mia mine Michelle
    Domingue I'm true to one
Mine mere Michelle
    Domingue there is but one

Sweet Michelle Domingue, daughter of us all,
though how many of us knew, truly?

The story is told by Mongolian elders that some
twenty-odd years ago a message was sent down from
Mt. Darjeeling to Bombay that a woman child was to
be born in America as God's daughter cum
messenger. Born of wealthy white parents, an only
child, she was brought up against a backdrop of Ivy
League well-to-do and moneyed Americans.

It is said that she was bred of the finest Colonial
stock, why the Domingue line of course (duh-ming,
rhymes with "sting"). It is also said that her great-
great grandfather Otto Domingue married a
Washington and that her great-great grandmother

came from a direct line of Washingtons and Franklins, all the way back to George and Ben. Michelle Venus Domingue has the blood of the founding fathers.

Far less is concretely known about the earlier Domingue breed. They are of course French in origin. Great-great-great-great grandfather was General Vulcan Hephaestus Domingue of the French Foreign Legion, best known for knocking the nose off of the Sphinx.

God was quiet though, God was quiet that day. There wasn't much to say. We the people didn't know nothin anyway, we just happened to be praying the same communal prayer

And Venus was her name, Michelle Venus Domingue. Oh praises to the merciful and potent Cosmologist. Oh praises on high...

Introduction

I've wondered the same thing myself: Is she telling the truth, maybe a half-truth? Or is she completely out of her mind, and this whole story just made-up, fictional?

This introduction won't clear up the nagging questions you the reader may have. The elusive Michelle Domingue has a knack for evading the simplest of questions. Like how old is she today or where does she live now and is she ministering to the people and where are those great admiring throngs now?

I met Michelle Domingue a few times in two different California locations before I agreed to put my name on her book. The first meeting was in a tiny outlaw border town one and a half hours east of San Diego. A town of 200 census-counted legal U.S. residents and a dusty desert hot springs motor lodge. We met in the hot springs bar.

There are at least five locals in that small drinking hole at all times, and usually a few motel guests. It was late June and it was about 100 degrees out. I ordered a drink and sat next to a woman who I thought was a local. She looked like she'd been around the block, literally. She said her name was Michelle Domingue, and explained that she wasn't from here, she was passing through, waiting for the next Greyhound. I told her I wasn't a local either, I was a musician on the road heading for my next gig, in Flagstaff, Arizona.

She must've taken a liking to me, because she opened right up and started telling me this incredible and unbelievable story. To be honest, I didn't believe a single word, the whole bit about her being some celebrity holy person or something. I didn't believe her, but I was absolutely fascinated and taken with her storytelling. If this gal was passing me a pack o' lies, they were really well-told lies. And she was such an eccentric character. I couldn't tell if she was drunk, completely mad, or — gulp! — telling me a wild and weird tale of her own life.

We exchanged mailing addresses and I promptly lost hers. However, half a year later I got a postcard from Michelle Domingue with a postmark from Dateland, Arizona. All she said was she would be in Los Angeles soon, and would I meet her at the Hotel Roosevelt on Hollywood Boulevard on such a date at such a time? That was it. Seemed weird, but I was curious enough to do it. And I guess I wanted to see if she was real — you know, not some road mirage I made up in my head.

We met in the lobby. Ordered drinks and sat in soft lounge chairs near the baby grand. A piano player had been hired by the hotel to play muzak versions of the 1960s and '70s hit parade. It was distracting.

When Michelle Domingue arrived she had a paper bundle under her arm and plopped it down on the table in front of me. She said she'd finished a book of her memoirs. She'd written out that whole story she'd told to me last year at the desert hot springs motor lodge. The whole story of how she'd become a messiah overnight, how she'd been hounded by the media, and this love story through it all. I told her I'd love to read it, and maybe I could pass it on to some folks who might want to publish it. Maybe I could help out somehow in some small way.

She said I could, and that's when Michelle Domingue asked me to put my name on the book as author. I'm still kind of embarrassed about it. And shocked that I agreed. I didn't understand at the time why she was so adamant about me doing it. Maybe I still don't. It's weird, I didn't write this book, but — whatever... I agreed to help out, and this is my way of helping, I suppose. Each quarter I send a royalty check to a room upstairs at the Hotel Congress in Old Tucson; that's our agreement.

I haven't seen her for a few years now. But the letters and checks I've sent to her don't come back to me, and I figure she's got a right to her privacy after all she's been through. It's up to you whether you want to believe her story as truth or not. Frankly, I'm not so sure I do myself.

Cindy Lee Berryhill
Encinitas, California
June 1999

Chapter One

It was the middle of autumn, the air was already getting a little cold and crisp around the edges. The summer constellations were dripping over the western seaboard, and Orion and the Pleiades were peeking up above the midnight east. This is probably my favorite time of year, why I don't know, perhaps because my mother died in the fall, years ago, which left me with a quiet, sometimes perfect longing.

It's been that longing that's moved me from town to town, from job to job, from woman to man. My life has been likened to that of a dust bowl days farmer, rambling, searching, gambling my dreams, using my wits, my street savvy. Now my daddy of course did pay for my excursions, but once I had a job at a candy store, saved up $500 and used it to pay for my shopping sprees. And many sprees I had until my daddy sent me away. I've often wondered if Daddy didn't want me around. Somehow I knew, if only intuitively, that I embarrassed him deeply. I didn't look like a Beverly Hills-ette should.

Nor did I look Colonial enough for Mommy and Daddy's winter world in Connecticut. Which I might say is where I was born. Brought forth from that cold cruel climate of the east. Summers took the family to Beverly Hills, California, and shopping malls, and loads of print dresses and still more disfavor from my father. I can still remember that lazy summer day I strode down our stony stair steps to the pool grounds. Father was down there with some dubious-looking clients. Father often worked with the department store underground, a mysterious clan of underworld figures distinguished by their expensive taste in clothing and a most peculiar body odor. A sort of toxic greasy stench like they'd eaten a lot of fatty beef and cheap steak sauce.

However, one man struck me as different. He smelt of apricot shampoo and wore it all over his sporty California suit. He wasn't particularly attractive, but it was his smell that lured me like a cat to milk, a boy to a drugstore. That day I made sure to wear my tightest and most expensive-looking dress. The fact was I looked incredible, I felt like Audrey Hepburn in *Breakfast at Tiffany's*, complete with diamond tiara, black gloves to the elbow, gorgeously sparkling rhinestone necklace and bracelet to match. I looked without a doubt stunning.

It's that last stone stair step does it to me every time, and, well, I tripped and fell, stumbling into the lime-colored rectangular pool. My father whirled about, his eyes falling. Oh, he was devastated indeed. The apricot-scented cutie leaned over the pool and gave me a gallant hand, pulling me out of the aqua depths. I knew my plan would work. I knew that this little stunt could make him mine. And indeed, as I looked into his iridescent blue cuff links and saw the reflection of those lovely brown eyes staring desirously back at me, Michelle Domingue, I was sure of the plan's effectiveness. I also knew I would never have my father's respect again. Ever. It was the black elbow gloves, they were a bit much. Since then, much to my chagrin, father has excommunicated me. I've had to grin and bear it and make it on my own in the months since then, since that sunny yet inwardly unsunny day.

So it was autumn. Father had flown me out east, shipped me south, railroaded me north, driven me west. West most recently. And it was here, west, not long ago at all, that I discovered the real romantic potential L.A. had in store for me, Michelle Domingue. It was the priceless age of 22. And it was autumn, it was cool, and it was the end of Father and the beginning of me, Michelle Domingue, and the beginning of... romance.*

---

* I particularly like the way I phrased that last sentence. Take a good look at it and read it over a few times. Good. I don't know who it reminds me of but it does remind me of some famous woman author, I can't think of her name. But anyway, I think that last sentence was structured quite well. Actually, it's reminiscent of the way my Aunt May writes her letters, oh she's a wonderful correspondent, it's obvious she's well-read. She wrote me a letter once just explaining the sounds she heard while sitting in her recliner chair, things like faucets dripping, children playing, the house creaking, her stomach growling. It was a work of art, truly.

It was the middle of autumn (oh I used this already, I'll use another). It was fall, halfway between hot summer and cold winter. The weather was turning chilly, I was twenty-two and in Beverly Hills. I was begging for jobs. I'd filled out over three applications that day and was on my last leg. Then...somewhere in the Chinese vase department of Neiman-Marcus, I expired. Temporarily. Things just went blurry, then fuzzy. I dropped my application and pencil mid-sentence, Chinese vases began to spin, the women's department sold clothes upside down. Fade to black.

Something was touching me, tugging at me. I blinked my eyes, my God. Before me was the apricotish young man from my father's poolside meetings. I slapped his face.

"How dare you!" I shouted. "How dare you push me down like that!"

I figured this ploy would make others think I was victimized and pushed, rather than falling by my own means out of pure poor-woman-like exhaustion.

"And what do you mean by putting this application for employment in my hand? Do you know who I am?"

"Frankly my dear, I don't give a damn," he said, pushing himself up from his knee, giving me the once-over and striding off.

Yes, it was most definitely autumn, crisp cool Beverly Hills autumn. That longing pounded throughout my every vein, as I collected myself, grabbed my application papers, and pushed through the gawking moneyed crowd.

"Hey you," I shouted. "Hey, stop that man, he took my purse. Stop that man that smells like apricot."

I quickly and cleverly stuck my purse/bag down my dress. The men's department loved it. I loved that the men's department loved it.

"Where the hell do you think you're going with my purse!"

I caught up with Mr. Apricot just as he was exiting, and motioned to the doorman.

"Grab him, he's got something of mine."

He shrugged politely.

"I'm sorry ma'am, I just do doors."

I stood there a moment and looked at him real good, shot him 99 angry dart thoughts, then I ran on. I lost my man in the multi-level parking lot.

"O.K., hey Mr. Apricot, forget it, you just go on ahead without me and forget it..."

Well, there he was in front of me.

"I don't need yourself obstructing my way."

"Oh yeah you do," he interrupted. "You've been chasing my obstruction for five years now."

"Help. Help this man is raping me, help, rape!" I yelled with a fervor unequaled. It was only seconds before a goon squad, three hearty-looking men, came promptly to my rescue.

"Mr. Apricot, is this woman harassing you?" one asked. The other grabbed my arm and began pulling me, separating me from my so secret love.

"No, no," he chuckled with a deeply patronizing flair. "Just funning, the lady and I are on our way to dinner."

"To dinner?" I queried loud and forceful. "I never, never..."

I never realized what happened till it happened, the three hearty fellows had me down on the grime grease ground in a split-second pretzel lock. I looked to them meekly.

"Oh yeah, I just forgot for a minute. Dinner."

Once I complied they of course let me go, helping me to my feet.

"Kyle, Clark, Ken, back off." Apricot's voice boomed its authority. "Back to the men's department, back to those ties."

"Yes sir." You see they all responded as one unified voice, saluted my soon-to-be "my" Mr. Apricot.

I straightened my glasses and followed my Mr. Marcus obediently to his 1995 Targa. This was not my idea of a romantically glorious re-meeting, quite the contrary. If he'd only done as I'd wished my plan was truly brilliant, I was to chase him for several days and then, when I got his hopes up, dump him. We would have talked deeply, urgently, passionately while standing over the bubbling oozing ore of the La Brea Tar Pits, strolling the grounds gazing at ancient fossilized saber-toothed tigers, while an age-old bond grew into cognition between us. He could have compared my frame to that of the La Brea Woman. Her Cro-Magnon frame peering at us from behind tourist-proof glass. Yes, we probably had been here before, long long ago. Something about the plastic mammoth behind the chain link fence sitting plastically still in the inky black muck rang an archaic bell. If only it would just come clear to me. And then he would say to me, "Darling, what's happening to us? I feel so, so...so primitive, I'm so hungry for you and for that mammoth." And I would say, "Don't hold back, let yourself go, but wait just a coupla minutes, I'll drive us to a Motel 6 on Sepulveda." Then we would have drunk motel room coffee and drunk water out of motel room plastic cups and gone down the hall and gotten motel lobby ice cubes. Oh God, that was my dream, but instead here I was slavishly driven to dinner in Mr. Right's Targa. I didn't say a damn word as he drove us through that shivery middle mid-autumn night. Down Wilshire, past our past (the Tar Pits), past the good theaters into Hollywood, armpit of the basin.

I'm no fan of Movieland. I had a traumatic experience there as a child. On the long drive from Connecticut to Hollywood, Daddy kept talking to me, telling me how we were going to see movie stars walking up and down the streets just like us. I could hardly wait.

In fact, I only went to the little girl's room twice the entire trip. I didn't want to slow us down. With all the hype and buildup my parents hard-sold me, we saw not a one star. I, needless to say, was devastated. Father tried to perk me up by buying me a little toy poodle named John Wayne, but to no avail. This did nothing but reflect badly on him, from then on I thought of all parents as stupid and insensitive. Father still owns JW to this day, though his coat has yellowed, and I still hate Hollywood. Well, there I was smack dab in the middle of it.

"I hope hamburgers will do," he said, looking innocent and apologetic as only a Neiman-Marcus manager can.

"Oh, yeah, fine," I huffed. Being the sensitive man he was, he sensed dissatisfaction in my tone and cut in.

"Now wait a minute." He pulled the car over, which was not wise, we were in the very dangerous intersection of La Cienega and Santa Monica. This added however to the sense of adventure, that I, Michelle Domingue, was just beginning to embrace. He stopped the car.

"Wait a fuckin' minute now—you been chasing me all over this fucking country and now you pull something like this."

His eyes sparkled with the heat of the moment. I knew I had him then, yes I did. I said nothing, just turned from my window to face him all big-eyed. Pausing, I said,

"Oh, I suppose, I suppose they would be just fine." I broke, bubbling. "But they better be the best."

"Oh honey," his smile grew, "they are indeed the best." And of course I, Michelle Domingue, knew just what he meant. I lit a cigarette and inhaled profoundly. Yes I did, I had him.

Ba Ba Boom!! Crunch.

My body convulsed helplessly forward, head abump and things all ablack. How long I was out I do not know, they told me later nearly nine minutes. But that nine minutes seemed a dreamful eternity, and it was certainly here I had my first real vision. Giant Havana Cigars floating over the Hollywood Holiday Inn, cubes flying over the Capitol Records building, then a thought flashed across my bruised surrealistic omen. A pure thought, uncensored, untouched — I dare say an instant of genius. The thought appeared in brilliant yellow caps just above the Roxy Nite Club. It read,

CHEESE IS THE MOLD OF LIFE.

"She's coming around, her eyes look all right."

Flash o blue, flash o yellow, flash o red, a psychedelic mish mash of go-go club lights, and a whirr of sound to boot.

"No, she can't be, that's impossible..."

I felt myself blinking.

"But doctor, her vital signs...were gone."

"Dammit youngun, I don't give a damn what your mechanical contraption says, she's coming around, she's fine."

My eyes finally adjusted and before me was one heavenly sight, a young angel, in white, with a stethoscope, a paramedic.

"Oh," I moaned, secretly feeling quite revived and refreshed. "Oh I can't quite breathe, would you—?"

"Why of course Ma'am," nodded the paramedic. And he proceeded to give me mouth-to-mouth like I never had it before. I had several orgasms.*

A half hour or so later, once the Targa had been carted off and Mr. Lovely Apricot and I were bandaged up and reported to be in excellent condition, we met our vehicular villain. He was a 19-year-old kid, turns out his scooter rear-ended us when he'd turned to kiss his girl.

Yes, it was a scooter, with a sidecar. Simply a wreck now, it had been a powerful little machine that could obviously deliver quite a wallop—which my dear frontal lobe could attest to. The scooter was towed off as well, which left the four of us there in the intersection, vehicleless. The kid offered his apology for the kiss to crash incident, which we

---

* I'd always been concerned as to whether I was multi or not. Now that I was I knew I'd never have to fake again. I was one of those special women now.

10

naturally accepted, and invited us to join him and his girl at their little nightclub.

The young man, I noticed, kept looking at me in an eerie manner. Finally, he pulled up his Dylanesque sunglasses and said,

"You know, for a minute or two there, you were dead."

"No," I of course corrected, "for a minute or two I was in heaven." And then the whole vision came flooding back.

CHEESE IS THE MOLD OF LIFE.

There was the first of that kind of silence that I was to aquaint myself with so well later. Perhaps at that time we all thought it to be just an accident. A verbal mistake of nature. A string of phenomenal syllables, a momentary freak of vocabulary, or even perhaps simple human genius.

"Let's just get out of here," I broke in, "I'm sick of this intersection."

We four hitched a ride on the back of a truck hauling plastic grapes. Mr. Apricot sat alone off to himself in a corner, and I knew something was eating at him. So I approached.

"Are you all right?"

"I suppose," he managed to get out.

"Is it your car?" I asked.

"No," he pouted.

"Is it no hamburger?"

"No."

"Is it an unlucky star?"

"No."

"From the car wreck, you might get a scar?"

"No."

"Then what the hell is it?

"Oh," he broke down, "I've always known there was something special about you, Michelle Domingue. Now it's clear as ever. The average person would have died with the bump on the head you received. But no, you wake up kissing on that doctor and start spouting some kind of mystic philosophy to us." His voice began to quiver and break. while I faded into another mental universe, receiving my second vision.

LIGHT IS NOT HEAVY.

I sputtered out, cutting off his monologue. Now Mr. Apricot broke down in tears. The others looked at me in silent awe.

"I'm sorry I said it, it just happened, I didn't mean..."

Mr. Apricot stopped me, throwing a hand-ful of plastic grapes poignantly across the truck floorboard.

"Oh damnit Michelle Domingue, don't apologize, you've got it, you're in your time. I'm just a shopkeeper in Beverly Hills, but honey (he looked me square in the third eye) you, you are some kind of..."

The girlfriend of Mr. Dark Dylan Glasses interrupted.

"You're some kinda nut—both of you. Sure as my name is Penelope. What'a ya mean, 'LIFE IS NOT HEAVY,' that's obvious, that's stupid."

"Penelope," Mr. Dark Glasses came to the rescue —a man of both truth and understanding—"sometimes it is the most obvious which is overlooked."

Penelope had no time to respond, for the truck o grapes had come to a halt in front of Mr. Glasses' night club. Penelope, however, thenceforth looked at me with a curiosity that was kept at a highly calculated and distrusting distance.

A neon light blinked and winked before us. It blinked out its message to Cahuenga Boulevard: CLUB. Unknowingly, I was about to step into a world that would change my world as I knew it to be —how was I to know that I would soon be a humble servant of the people—oh, to turn back the tide pre-accident, pre-vision. My call word was very soon to be "I vant to be alone," unheeded, unheard. Perhaps it wasn't a word, yet a Word.

A cool chill fell over me, what a gorgeous mid-October evening. A swollen cheesy yummy moon was creeping up over the eastern skyline. I could barely see it through all the atmospheric disturbances of the city, all the sulfur and neon lights. But it was there, sure enough, a moon only midautumn could born. And I knew on a deep esoteric level that somewhere in the San Joaquin Valley of California people were picking grapes and rejoicing to that very same harvest moon. In fact we humankind were all gazing at that very same moon...everywhere in California.

"Are we going in, or just standing around?"

Penelope snapped me out of my personal utopia, she had a finely tuned talent for doing that. Yet I, Michelle Domingue, was not yet ready to face what I knew I must face, sooner or later.

"Look," I blurted out. "I'm going to the little girls' room, I'll join the three of you in there."

Holding my breath, clutching at my stomach, for a terrible wave of nausea had descended upon me, I made a fast break for the women's room. My timing was good and I flushed the symptoms of self-fear down into the Los Angeles sewage systems, to travel and transverse where it all does and to eventually awaken with the light of day somewhere in Santa Monica Bay. I felt better already and would have left then had it not been for the embarrassing grunts and groans of pleasure just outside my stall door. I suppose they didn't know I was there. Because they were going at it with a ferocity that intimidated even me, Michelle Domingue.

Well I wasn't going to wait forever, and heaven knows I wasn't going to wait for the woman to orgasm. I could be there all night. Then again, he could be one of those wham bam types. For once in my life, I prayed he was. He wasn't though, he was damn sensitive, so I, taking my embarrassment in my hands, courageously strode out of the stall door.

14

"Excuse me."

"Hey don't worry 'bout it sister."

Oh it was two women, they realized my squea-mishness.

"Hey don't worry about it," she reinforced.

So I didn't, the three of us ended up talking feminist politics for an hour there in the ladies' room. They impressed me with their political astute-ness and punk-looking attire.

"Hey," said one, "don't you know what kinda place this is?"

"No."

"That's what I thought, honey," she said, giving my simple, yet expensive-looking outfit a good look.

"Do you jam, do you jerk, honey we'll show you the latest dancing quirk. Goes like this."

They showed me, Michelle Domingue, the lat-est dance steps so I could be prepared for hipness, and I left them there in the Club restroom with my third vision:

LIFE IS YES, YES IS LIFE. LIFE IS NO, NO IS LIFE. LIFE IS A BUNDLE OF YES'S AND NO'S AND MAYBE A FEW MAYBE'S OR SO.

They proceeded to kiss my hand with tears in their eyes and I left them there like that.

I needed my man, needed to find my man. I groped through the damp dim joint and was gouged by elbows from every angle. I was swimming through a mass of humanity. The club was jammed tight with an overflow of bodies. Mirrors on all four walls made us appear to be throngs. I felt as though I'd been cast in a Cecil B. DeMille film, but knew better. The music was harshly loud and oppressive and I was waving my hands in the air frantically shouting for my baby Apricot, when a man's arm grabbed at my waist from behind.

"Oh baby," I heaved with relief, "I've been looking for you."

We stared at each other in the midst of the fevered multitudes with a love that cut through all the crap.

"This is for you," said Apricot, handing me a card and a note. It read: "You're the one, yes you are, I think I've found my lucky star."

We grabbed at each other passionately and kissed for nearly a minute. This was truly the romance of the century like the Brownings, John and Yoko, Dante & Beatrice. Oh god, we had found one another. He adjusted the gauze bandage on my head.

"It becomes you, really."

"No," I said.

"No, really, it looks like a turban."

"No."

"Yeah, you look like a messiah..."

It was supposed to be a joke, but no one laughed. He stopped. For one split second the crowd stopped, the music ceased. A moment later the clubsters were again shoving us from either side. trying to get to the musical group thrashing it out with a sweaty fervor on stage.

"Look," his eyes gleamed, "I don't know why, but I think I love you."

We touched hands with a pure fiery power, our fingers wound around one another like green garden ivy.

"But damn, Michelle Domingue, you could never belong to me, you belong to the nameless faces now, to the world. I don't know what the hell that accident did to you, or me for that matter. But you got something kid, take it from me I know, I've lived in Beverly Hills, land of 'Special Somethings,' all my life. You got things to teach us humans — Gawd it's hard to say, but your lover, sweetie, is this human race."

My beloved Apricot was of course right. We held each other with a sweaty flaming power reserved only for the desperate. Our love seemed hopeless and I held him there, tightly, soulfully, while I still could.

"Blah, blah, blah..."

Someone was speaking over the PA system, the band had finished, and someone was announcing something.

"Er, blah of blah blah...Michelle Domingue."

My name! A coupla polite kids clapped.

"Get up here, Michelle darlin'."

It was Mr. Dark Dylan Glasses, damn him. I let go of my beloved Apricot, the right side of my face felt numb from pressing tight to his.

"Get up here, Michelle Domingue, you knucklehead, teach us something."

I walked forward, through the parting seas of people. Some of the leather coat types started shouting things like, "bring back the band," and "fuck off, Michelle Domingue." Of course I didn't take it personally, my great-grandfather was once a great vaudeville star and had taught me everything I knew about tap dancing and hecklers.

I climbed the stairs to the stage and approached the microphone. I was admittedly scared, I hadn't performed since my dance recital days as a child. I said "hello." Some people laughed, someone else threw a cabbage at me. I gained all the strength of character I could muster and broke into "Mississippi Mud." It felt good to sing and dance again.

"Hey, hey Uncle Fud it's a treat to beat your feet on the Mississippi Mud."

Oh God, the crowd started booing. I immediately dove into "Old Man River, it keeps a rollin'." Proceeded into a soft-shoe. Someone threw a shoe at me. It hit me on the leg. It stung. I stopped.

"Just stop it and shuddup," I shouted.

The crowd grew silent. I was at a loss, I didn't know any more songs, suddenly my fourth vision came to me, clear as plastic, and the words:

A ROCK IS A ROCK, A DIAMOND IS A ROCK, A FOSSIL IS A ROCK, A GEM IS A ROCK, A PIECE OF COAL IS A ROCK, A ROCK IS A ROCK.

The audience grew stone silent. I could hear a few cars whirr by in the one a.m. autumn. A dog was barking across the street, a bum was picking through garbage outside the club door. Then, a sob broke loose. Then a few more, someone put roses at my feet, someone else took a bar rag and began wiping my patent leather shoes.

Oh my God, what was happening? And then the capper. Involuntarily, as though vomiting, I spit out:

A MOUNTAIN IS A PILE OF ROCKS.

By then, I'd say 75 percent of the club was bawling loudly, releasing their deepest fears, experiencing their greatest joys. A man from the audience brought me a gauze robe and wrapped it about me, a woman brought me a wreath of dried wild flowers which had been a table setting, she had carefully woven them together, and then set them atop my head. Then several people in the bar crowd lifted me up off the stage and paraded me out into the middle of Cahuenga Boulevard. Traffic came to a standstill. It seemed that people came out of the woodwork. Suddenly in a span of mere minutes there was a multitude. I was set on the hood of a parked Mazda. "Speak, speak," they all shouted.

A moment of waiting was needed for the crowd to settle and quiet. My baby Apricot pushed his way to the front and gave me the thumbs up. I waited another minute, nothing really came to mind.

"It all started in a 50-watt radio building, in Bakersfield California... I was ten..."

No, no, no, no, no, no, they all screamed, "Tell us the real thing." I was wondering if I should or could fake it, maybe I could say, God Is Love. I tried it.

"God Is Love."

No, NO, No, no, no, no, they scolded. "Tell us..." and they all smiled and waited. And I, being Michelle Domingue, closed my eyes real tight and waited also.

"Hey, fuck this, I'm not a dog that barks on command. Fuck this. What do you want me to say? Fuck..."

It came up like the low rumble of moog synth. Always, always without warning.

"Get back, get back from her."

Someone was pulling at me and my Apricot's voice rang out over the voices of the many.

"Leave her alone..."

Cameras were zoom-lensing in on me, everybody was pressing in closer waiting for the word. But over and above all this came the low penetrating throb. The gathering group merely an undertone constant.

"Stand back," I pleaded.

An immediate hush rang over the boulevard. Something involuntary was beginning to happen to me, it seemed to come from my very womb. Cradle of life. Something was happening!

I opened my eyes. I crossed my legs. I felt it moving down down, and held tight.

"I gotta go."

The crowd let out a simultaneous sigh of disappointment. Someone in a big flop hat with Birkenstock sandals and a Grateful Dead T-shirt and bells asked if I had to go number one or number two.

"That's disgusting," I chided.

"Yes," the hippie volleyed, "but natural."

Mr. Apricot promptly took me from my throne and escorted me to a shadowy alley.

"I won't look," he promised, "my eyes are shut."

"Look, don't bother, Apricot, I can't go anyways without paper in my hand."

His eyes darted about the alley, finally he attacked a glint a few paces away.

"Here," he shoved a Snickers Bar wrapper into my hand.

"I don't think I can use this since they changed the paper to this sort of plastic stuff, what kind of paper is this anyway?, it's not really paper."

"I don't know baby, just use it."

I tried to use it.

"See, it just doesn't wipe...no," I shook my head. "It doesn't work."

His head was still turned away, but I could sense his impatience with me.

"Well, then use your damn hand!"

"Absolutely not!" I said with resolution.

My poor Mr. Apricot, he huffed and puffed, finally...

"Well then use my goddamn hand, I won't look."

"Mr. Apricot," I was shocked. "That's very noble of you."

I did my business and in minutes we were back out in front of the throngs. Something had come to me while releasing. My number 5 vision. And I was proud and happy to present it to the awaiting faces. Besides, I was ready to get it over with. It was all getting just a bit much. I stood back upon my Mazda perch, everyone did an ECU and I spoke.

THE DAY IS YELLOW, THE NIGHT IS BLUE, THE DAY IS YELLOW AND BLUE, THE NIGHT IS BLUE AND YELLOW.

There was a moment of extreme nothingness, perfect vacuum. For a while there was no gravity, no sound. For a moment we were all John Glenn. Then everything broke and I woke into a barrage of flashbulbs, poking, extending microphones and a billion unanswerable questions.

Questions like:

Who is Michelle Domingue?

Where did you get your outfit?

Why didn't your press agent send me a bio?
Where does your power come from?
Do you love your father and mother?
Is God black or white?
Was Revelations drug-induced?
Who's this year's Academy pick?
Do you love the president?
Do you menstruate?
Are you the second coming?
(I particularly liked that one.)
"No," I retorted, "I'm multiple now."
(I felt a sense of pride and thought of the
      American flag.)
Did you get this way through Est?
Are you a Scientology clear?
Do you believe in God, Baba Ram Das,
      Beatles, Jesus, the nine-fold muse?
Do you believe one can truly be monogamous?
Are you from another planet?
What is the concealed holy name of God?
Is mankind worth keeping?
Will it be the plutonium bomb?
When's your next film?
Will you be suing the *Enquirer*?
Will you mate?
Who is the originator of origins?
"Well..."

My fingers stroked my upper lip dramatically.
"I...don't know."

I took Mr. Apricot's hand, jumped off the Mazda and walked away from Cahuenga Boulevard. I knew that would hold them whilst us two lovers made our getaway. I was ready for our first two-minute kiss.

Chapter Two

It was one of those nights and early early mornings in mid-fall you can never ever forget. Mr. Apricot and I bared the chill by huddling together like sea gulls in the Santa Monica sand. The big fat-face moon was just a-smiling to us from the western skies as we sat arm in arm on the yellowy lunar-stroked beach. The ocean waved and rippled and foamed at the mouth and tided and stretched way over the horizon. I could trace a good extent of L.A. County to the north and south through the glittery shoreline. It curved slightly semicircular around us as though leaning towards a hot fire. Little blinky lights here and there dotted the inky drink, we watched them silently as they took hours to move from one dark water place to another.

"Mr. Apricot," I asked out of the blue after several hours of quiet had passed, "do you think this is love?"

We looked piercingly into one another's eyes, searching without seeking, looking without peering.

"I only know that I want you, Michelle Domingue, more than I ever wanted my manager's position at Neiman-Marcus."

"Oh," I said lovingly. I knew that meant a lot.

We kissed this time for nearly three minutes, maybe a record. His mouth was hot and wet and slimy and tasted a little bit salty. Then he pulled away.

"I can't, I really can't do this." He looked at me with a longing that bespoke thousands of years of bad karma.

"Oh my darling Michelle Domingue, I feel so wrong. She's been the center of my life, of my attentions, for so long. Well before I met you in your Audrey Hepburn dress and gloves. I just can't turn my back on her, do her wrong like this. And yet, I want to spend every waking moment with you."

"What about your sleeping moments?" I asked, concerned.

"Those have been reserved for all the dream She's, the dream department stores I've ever wanted to have, ever wanted to hold, to... it's just a sexual thing, I'm a man and can't help my feelings."

Yes, deep inside I knew of his ambitious sexual desires. This man had to take every department store in Beverly Hills. That was a man for you. I also knew that I, a mere human, a mere woman, a mere womb, a mere cunt, a mere five and a half square feet could never compare with *her*. Her, in all her marbled glory an easy 100,000 square feet. There was so much more to *her*. Perhaps she was even 120,000 square feet, counting her executive offices. Tears welled up in my eyes for the first time in this book.*

Mr. Apricot held me and brushed my tears away. We said nothing more. He made his hand into a sort of cuplike shape and formed it against my right breast, giving me that 'does that feel good?' look. I wasn't quite sure, it felt a lot like wearing a one-cup brassiere. Then he repeated the procedure with his other hand and my left breast. Now we've got a full bra. We sat there like that, unmoving for five or six minutes until he decided to try something else. I touched the bulge in his pants, but soon became aware that the bulge was his belly roll and moved lower. Yes, here was Mr. Apricot's love thing, the thing that could potentially transmit bad diseases. Yet, I knew better with my Mr. Apricot. Within seconds we both had our clothing off and folded and were rolling passionately in the damp night sand. We rolled about 50 yards down the beach, then rolled back next to our clothes. Then we kissed again.

"Do you wanna do it?" I inquired.

He nodded affirmatively. We didn't have a condom so I found a piece of Glad Wrap and used it

---

* Note how I had the man cry several times earlier in the story, and waited for the woman, me, Michelle Domingue, to cry. I just wanted to demonstrate something. I think it's good to make political points here and there, I think it's an artist's responsibility.

effectively. It was so romantic. Just as he put his thing in my thing I had an orgasm, rolled over and fell asleep. All night the repetitive sound of the waves lulled me deeper into that black hypnotic sleep. Suddenly without much warning it was morning. Someone was tapping me, waking me. I became aware that I was covered from head to toe with newspaper.

"Ma'am, you'll have to be moving along. We don't allow naked people to sleep on the beach."

It was a cop. Then I noticed, it hit me like a rock thrown at me by my own sister. My Apricot was gone and nowhere in sight. I knew somehow that he'd been tortured and torn by his own deep passionate love and desire for me and yet also the security of his beloved department store. I wondered seriously whether my own true love would ever return to me and for the first time in this writing I felt a faint instance of depression. The officer kicked me right out of it by kicking me lightly on the rump.

"Ma'am, please don't make a problem for us..."

"Officer, sir," I cut in, "I would be happy to oblige, if you would please not mind turning seaward, I am a lady and need to dress unviewed."

"Yes Ma'am," he responded, turning away.

"You got a wife?" I asked.

"Yes Ma'am," he retorted.

"You got a kid?"

"Yes, Ma'am."

"You got a dog?"

"Yes Ma'am."

"You got a radar range?"

"Yes Ma'am."

"You got a dee-vorce lawyer?"

"No Ma'am!"

"Then whatcha doin' looking at my nekkedness out of the side of your sunglass?"

"Yes, Ma'am!"

Of course I knew no man on earth could resist my form.

I was just combing out the one teeny knot in my hair—another officer had arrived, bringing us coffee, we were chatting it up when I noticed a young man running in our direction. He was doing the best he could trotting through the deep Santa Monica sand, and, in his haste, fell numerous times. He finally breathlessly dragged it to our beach dune and collapsed. He lay there, on the ground, pointing over and over to his mouth. The officers and I looked at one another bewildered, sipping our coffee. A third officer joined us and for a few minutes we munched donuts and waited for the youngish man to speak. I finally gave in and knelt by his side.

"Would you like a glazed? A maple bar?"

No, he shook his natted hairy head. I gave him the last of my weak coffee. He slurped at it and then took it down in one fell gulp. Then I motioned for him to come closer. He didn't seem able to, so I moved toward him. He had a five-day old whisker and a very foul smell. Lifting his head a bit, he tried to speak to me, Michelle Domingue, in some kind of Morse Code message. He spat and choked and breathed out a cluster of garbles. His breath was that of rotted teeth. I held my breath and listened, finally a few words made sense.

"Hollywood party... in your honor... Beverly Wilshire Hotel..." The young raggedy messenger gasped loudly, so loudly I was embarrassed for a moment. Then quiet. His message conveyed, he passed on into another world, another life, another someplace.

Police vehicles have always intrigued me, they always remind me of lovely merry-go-rounds, with all their flashing and loud alarms and men in funny costumes. I sat to my officer's right, up front. It made me think of the swan chairs, the two-seat arrangements on the merry-go-rounds. Whee.

"The Beverly Wilshire," my companion muttered, "nice mo-tel."

It was so very nice of this gentleman, this officer of the law, to give me an escorted lift to the big Hollywood party in my honor. And what was it going to be like once I got there? What was fame like anyway? I would soon find out.

Oh, it was a beautiful day, a perfect autumn noon. The sun hot, not quite to the zenith—for in fall the sun never reaches the sky's apex. It was then I noticed the sun was not in the right place, we were heading north. Which, I must say, was the wrong way.

"Officer," I asked nicely, "I think we're going the wrong direction. Shouldn't we be heading *east*?"

"Oh no problem there hon, just wanted to show you a good time an' a good view. We're going by way of Mullholland."

"Oh."

Something smelt fishy. We wove in around and through the ancient hills of chaparral, past 405, past all the fancy homes of stars and great bankers along Hollywood's most famous lovers' lane. I kept wondering how long it would take to do the whole route from end to end. Leo Carillo State Beach to Cahuenga Pass, the whole 21 miles. Could take days at the rate this guy was driving, and what was I thinking anyway? I had another fish to fry. We suddenly pulled off the road and gravel-crackled to a halt. We were in a shady alcove overlooking the San Fernando Valley.

"I'm sorry I didn't bring a picnic basket," he said. I checked my watch several times, tapped my toe loudly so he'd get the hint. No going.

"Look," I interrupted the swishing leaves and chirping birds, "I gotta get to that party. I got no time for socializing, no time to tell you I don't wanna be here, no time for picnics, no time for tweeting birds, no time for rape." I tried to put my point across gently yet decisively.

"Oh come now," he coaxed, "just a little rape, no big deal — you don't even have to fight, OK?"

My officer had a smile on his face showing small deep lines of age. Probably too much sun, too much SoCal sun brought out those deep kinds of lines.

"Look," I said firmly, letting the middle-aged man down gently, "absolutely not. It's just too messy, too much paperwork involved, my father would never pay for the attorneys. And frankly, I've got too much fame and notoriety to take the time off for courtroom hullaballoos. I know," I looked at him deeply, "you're disappointed. But honey have you ever tried a different approach?"

He grabbed me, pushing me domineeringly down in the seat and clasped his hands around my throat.

"Oh honey no no." I was so embarrassed for him. I tried to hold back a deep, resounding belly laugh. His whole expression dropped, his hands went limp. I scooted back up into a respectable sitting position.

"Oh look," I tried to perk him up a bit, "look, there is a better way. You're just too animal that way. Just too much, and not much of a turn-on. I'm so sorry."

He just sat there all glum, the high Bel-air breeze hummed through the cracked windows of the patrol car. Then like a wave like a storm like a...well like a thought from nowhere, came a thought from nowhere. I couldn't hold it back.

YOUR GRANDFATHER'S CLOCK HAS A TICK ON IT.

My officer broke down in sudden spurting sobs. Tears seemed to shoot from his pinched eyelids.

"That's it! That's it! Oh God I understand now. Oh Michelle, that's why I've been a failure all these years. Thank you, thank you! My grandfather was a rapist, a smelly rat that hated me, an all-around bad guy." He kissed my hand, a joy shot out from his face where tears once had stood, flew out over the Hollywood hills, swooped down the San Fernando Valley and disappeared to the north towards Bakersfield towards McFarland towards Delano. And I thought of the joy that someone picking cotton outside Tulare might be capturing this very moment. My officer hugged me, wet with tears, and my trance ended.

"Oh, thank you, I'm healed," he repeated again and again. "I'll never have to rape again—ever. I'm healed."

"I'm so glad, darling — now would you kindly motor me to my Hollywood wingding?"

"Yes, Ma'am, anything."

He looked at me good, real good, in a different sort of way now, in a deep awed existential light, the way Jack Kerouac probably looked at Neal Cassady. "You're a goddess," he breathed.

It took us nearly an hour to get down the hill into Beverly Hills, what with all the traffic and swarms of admirers outside the Beverly Wilshire Hotel. But in that hour's time I thought deeply, brilliantly, of many many things. My officer seated next to me was a shining beacon of radiant light. What a transformation he'd made. Perhaps there was a way for me to package, merchandise, these genius quips, these surges of mine so that all could receive. Like Norman Vincent Peale, Robert Schumann, or LSD I could with the wave of my tongue transform lives, change destinies. What was happening to me? I was as good as chocolate—perhaps better because I didn't have to be imported or mixed with sugar. I was as good as electricity or even Albert Einstein but still more marketable, being an attractive woman with a sharp sense of style and an outgoing personality, good body, that's the one thing Einstein missed out on. I, Michelle Domingue, was certain to meet many male stars, all the Warren Beattys, Richard Geres & John Does I would ever desire to meet. But — the thought flashed through my mind like a ribbon of two-ply toilet paper cleansing my hedonistic desires—I was to remain true to my love for my Mr. Apricot. I would give him time to crawl back to me and beg forgiveness. I understood.

The patrol car whined and burned through the crowds, lights all a-flash. I stepped from my black &

white chariot onto a red carpet escort. Flashbulbs flicked, cameras clicked, the crowd roared, I waved back. I smiled and brushed Santa Monica sand off my dress.

"Goodbye officer." I touched his hand, he touched mine, then we were torn apart by the tug-and-pull force of the riptide of people. It was like a big ocean of colors, of clothing and hair. How did they know about this? Was this real, was this for me, really? I deserved it, of course, I knew my brilliance and am not modest.

Suddenly a young boy of nine or ten rode by on a Sting Ray bicycle with a blue-and-silver-speck banana seat with butterfly handlebars. He picked a neatly rolled wad of paper out of his canvas bag and threw it, it landed and fell open at my feet. *Los Angeles Times*: "Miracle Maker Michelle Moves Mountains."

"What is this?" I exclaimed. "I've never yet moved a mountain, never yet."

One of my escorts leaned towards me and whispered, "I think they mean that figuratively, Miss Domingue, you know, you moved a mountain of people."

I was all enraged they were making me out to be something I was not. I was merely a brilliant God-inspired philosopher of phenomenal proportions. Not a messiah, never a mover of—my face flashed red—mountains.

"I am merely a brilliant God-inspired philosopher of phenomenal proportions," I said, "not a messiah, never a mover of mountains."

The crowd went hush and I huffed and puffed past them, past my escorts, past the big wide Beverly Wilshire doors into the lobby proper. And there on a lobby coffee table spread out all prim and proper were five or six well-known newspapers and periodicals with my name and face on them. *Newsweek*: "Michelle Domingue — Second Coming?" *Time*: "Second Coming — Michelle Domingue? *New York Times*: "Modern Day Messiah Found in Michelle Domingue." *Enquirer*: "I am the first-born of Messiah Michelle."*

I could take no more. I looked up, astonished, confounded — why me? And then I noticed a nice older woman sitting presentably in a lushly cushioned lobby sofa, deeply involved in her reading material — a book. *In and Out of Bed with a Modern Messiah, and the Theories of Compensation: Exclusive Information on Michelle Domingue* by...Mr. Apricot! I gasped, I choked, I coughed, I gasped again. I coughed again. The older woman ran to my aid.

"Honey, honey," she slapped my back, pumped my arms, threw her arms around my rib cage and

---

* *I know, it doesn't seem like all these things could have happened overnight. But this is how I remember it. Maybe I was asleep on the beach longer than I thought. Or maybe there was some kind of timewarp set up by the messiah messages.*

squeezed. She did it all. I however was not really choking, I was merely expressing amazement.

"I'm OK, I'm all right," I shouted, "really." She turned me upside down, she shook me, she opened my jaw and stabbed her finger in and around and through my mouth.

"Ugh, uh bbb whaw u-ee." She didn't understand, I didn't understand, what I was saying. Finally, breathing heavy and looking like a track star coming in fifth, she quit, fell back in the sofa.

"My, my," I admired, "you really know all those positions, don't you?"

She heaved and breathed. A reserved-looking gentleman strode by and gave us the once-over.

"I'm really all right, I was just taken aback by your reading material. May I take a look?"

She nodded yes to me. The book was on the coffee table. I approached and circled it as though it were my prey. There on the front was a drawing of a robed and haloed woman and a man (not unlike my Mr. Apricot) kissing in bed. How could he! How dare he? That scum, that slime. Maybe he never really cared. Maybe we never really were John & Yoko, Tracy & Hepburn. Maybe Michelle & Apricot will not be whispered on lips of lovers in days long to come. I broke down sobbing and fell upon the book. "Oh how could he, that scumface!" My dream shattered in an instant.

"Miss, miss," the old woman tapped me. "Please

don't mess my copy — you'll smudge. There there, yes the book moved me too. Particularly that part, the mad passionate lovemaking (that scum), such love (that creep), such desire (that shit), at the Griffith Park Observatory while gazing at the Horsehead Nebula.

Not only was that Apricot a scum a creep a shit, he was a liar.

"Kissing for hours..."

Exaggeration.

"She never knew such delight."

Perhaps, though the thought of it at an observatory disgusted me. Science and sex sounded so dirty.

She ran the pages past her fingers, then stopped and jabbed at some point in the book.

"It's so...well, sexy."

I was embarrassed. I could never admit now to who I was. Not now. Yet not knowing the emotional storm raging inside me, she read on:

> I unlatched Michelle Domingue's bra. I wondered if this flimsy piece of elastic was named after Tycho Brahe, the great astronomer, epic discoverer. I too had some discovering to do...
>
> The scientific equipment and the telescope and all transported us to other worlds. I felt like the mind of Arthur C. Clarke. I was falling, falling into her. I was

to explode to a hundred times my size, then the process would reverse all to implode, till I was a nothing in a sea of nothing. This is the world of the Black Hole and her magnetic fields were mercilessly pulling me in...

We did it rung by rung till we reached the mirror of the telescope proper. Oh God, great worlds, star clusters, nebulae where whole suns were being born, exploding into view. 'My God, I'm going blind!' I shouted.

The mirror was like a clear flat pancake, like a misplaced pond of ice. The two of us naked under the stars slithered slid skidded about the glass, bodies touching, hearts beating, minds blending. Michelle and I were one. It was then through the meeting of minds that I first envisioned my theories of compensation. The principles and laws flashed through my mind like a wild and alive computer screen. Michelle sensed what was happening, her mind acted as a battery. Grabbing pencil and paper I sat there scrawling, scratching out lines, numbers and words I had little control over and no understanding of. This was the handwriting of God itself.

Laws of Compensation

When a vacuum is created it is quickly filled.

There is no vacuum in the cosmos.

Vacuum is not a vacuum.

There is no such thing as nothingness.

There are particles that we are not even aware of, everywhere.

$$Y + X^2MC^2 \times XY^2 =$$
speed of light $\times XY^2$ etc. etc.

The universe is not expanding into nothingness, it is growing into a somethingness.

All materials minerals substances waves and thoughts are everywhere throughout the universe. There is nothing new under the sun, only combinations we have not thus far in recorded history been aware of.

My God, not only was my one true love a liar a scum and an all-American exploiter, he was also a genius! It was no wonder the two of us were brought together by fate or God or the law of attraction or karma or luck or whatever else there is to set your belief in. Two brilliant minds joining forces, coming together, perhaps we had some sort of mission, perhaps we were to rebuild the entire complex of Mattell toys located somewhere in the vast L.A. County area. God only knows. God knew. But until we were to come together and work as a powerful Maxwell Maltz mastermind I would have to confront Mr. Apricot about this book and slug him hard in the eye. The woman with the book read on, rambling, delighting in each new passage, I could take no more and was dead tired. So while the outside crowds pounded and cheered, while the old woman read, while my stomach churned cuz you may have noticed I hadn't eaten for some time, I fell gently, autonomously, asleep.

It was decorated all fancy expensive-like. Much like one of those gala ballrooms from some movie like *Gigi*. Someone forgot to inform me about the preferred attire, for I was still wearing my same dress. Lovely as it was, it had become rather mussed, and my hair a bit tossed from my hearty couch nap. The gifted new wunderkind movie director Eric Von Strideright had woken me up on his way into the party hall, realizing that I might miss out on all the wonderful compliments and "Michelle, you're a goddess"es that could be thrown my way. Strideright is such a dear. Perhaps we'll do a project one day. But not now, not as I look at the panorama of lights, yakking celebrities, banners of red white and blue, the three-foot-high cake in the shape of a cross with my name, Michelle Domingue, on it. Not now while I stand alone in a sea of stars considering my long lost love Mr. Apricot.

The crowd noises were piercing, and a music group the Alt Tent, a Dead Kennedys cover band, had come all the way down from Santa Cruz to play for the event. They were just finishing up a foot-tapping rendition of "California Uber Alles" when the singer began Blah diddy Blahing over the PA about something or other. And then I heard my name, Michelle Domingue. Things became real eerie quiet, real unnatural like that sick "Happy Birthday to You" when everyone smiles at you, *act overwhelmed, quiet.* The velvet drape curtains were rippling slowly back and forth in the Beverly Hills breeze. People were squishing down into velveteen and curled wood chairs. The enormous overhead chandelier in the shape of a banana tinkled and twinkled.

"Look, what time is it?" I asked. Because I suddenly remembered there was an 11:40 freight train heading out of town ready to pick up a load of grapes in Fresno. Maybe I'd jump it.

Someone answered, "It's birthday time!" Alt Tent started playing a punk rock version of "Happy Birthday" and five big dark-haired muscle shirt men wheeled a big fat cake in front of my face. How could I ever tell them, my fans, fans of Michelle Domingue, that it wasn't my birthday? This party was to herald my talents, not my birthday—which it wasn't. Everyone was clapping and I couldn't get a word in edgewise. Suddenly Don Pardoe's voice boomed out over the excited can't-barely-hear-a-thing level: "Michelle Domingue, do you want what is behind the curtain OR inside the cake that Carol Merrill is now showing?" Sure enough, Carol was right there waving her hand back and forth along the big fat cardboard cake. Everyone shouted, "Cake!"

So, "cake" it was.

Well, out came an Apricot, my Apricot, my baby Apricot, that scumbag that misled the literary world about my ways of sex.

He smiled a big cheesy, fruity Apricot smile at me.

"Michelle," he yelled, "Michelle baby, I quit my job at Neiman-Marcus. I'm due to make a million dollars off of book sales. I'm up for the Nobel Prize for my theories of the laws of compensation this year. You're fucking lovely, I'm fucking great, let's get the fuck outta here."

He jumped down from his cake perch, grabbed my arm, shoved a gawking Eric Von Strideright aside, and pushed me out into the night before I could say "geodesic dome house.' I could kill him and have his baby all at one time. Our affair, our passion was such a tumultuous one. He pushed me out into the Wilshire Boulevard night. There was fire in our touch, there was a volcano in my stomach. But this wasn't the time or the place to vomit. Yet that is what our love wanted for me, it was a burning churning hunk a hunk a burning-kinda love. The kinda love that made Elvis's hips go round. Apricot was still running, dragging me down the street. We ran down Rodeo Drive, past Gucci's, past all those little U.S. stores with big European names, down Santa Monica Boulevard, past Cahuenga up Sunset past the Denny's. We ran for hours and finally ended up somewhere in the Silverlake District. It felt so good, so right. I grabbed him and ran him south into Los Angeles proper, to—the train station.

"What are we doing here, Michelle Domingue?" He huffed and puffed and teetered, nearly passing out as he used his second-to-last breath to speak. Then used his last breath to light a cigarette.

I looked at him quizzically, not for any real reason, just because the word fit. The night had become a steamy hot one. We were standing next to the old train yard by the tracks. Rails of silver streaked moon-shiny from north to south. It was a good dark Kerouac hot hedonistic night.

Then I smiled. "God, I'm glad you got me out of there, Apricot baby. I was stuck." He responded well to this gesture by patting me on the calf twice, braiding my hair and promising to accompany me to a low grade "B" movie. "You gotta know how much I appreciate... This much." I grabbed the minus-three-drags Marlboro from his clinched Bogart lips, tossed it fervently to the ground, and with great feeling shoe-smashed it into the train yard rubble.

"That much, that much, Mr. Apricot is how much I appreciate my name smeared all over the pages of your fucking bestseller. Lies, all lies! You Bastard, you. You! It wasn't so much the sex, it wasn't so much the observatory, it wasn't so much the anything, but the lies. And by the way, you might be quasi-brilliant but your Laws of Compensation don't make sense."

Apricot got that astonished look on his shadowed face, his lit half looked so sharp and video-real in comparison.

"What?! I save you from that Hollywood hullabaloo and this is my reward? You always think you're smarter than me, Michelle Domingue."

"Well, ain't I?" I quipped.

He didn't answer, he just picked up the squashed ciggy, lit it, and stormed down the tracks, Tehachapis-bound.

"Hey you," I shouted, "if you're gonna leave me like that, don't go north, I'm gonna be catching the northbound train any minute now and I don't wanna run into you. With the way I'm feeling now I'd probably psychically make the train veer off the track and hit you, and I wouldn't want to do that until we went on one of those love problem psycho hanging plant 1980s-style talk shows and discussed in full the nature of our impasse."

"Fuck off!" he shouted, and kept walking north.

Me, a little louder: "Look Apricot, it's a bad night to be out, Mars is in Aries. The Dodgers lost yesterday."

But nothing seemed to be working, I tried 'em all. "You're repressing your anger—it'll come back. You'll probably have a heart attack any minute now or maybe a nervous breakdown, spontaneous combustion, wet your bed, phobic, you'll become a mass murderer if you don't come back here, you scumbag."

He kept walking. Apparently he wanted to commit suicide and become a zombie hypno member of the new SLA. That's all that said to me. Hell, he wasn't leaving Michelle Domingue, he was running out on his own life. I pitied his Godless soul.

"You'll rot in hell, Apricot. Ask for forgiveness. Jesus will forgive you."

That sleazeball. He was still out there storming north on the tracks. It was getting too dark to see him. Perhaps, perhaps I could help the poor soul. No, I didn't want him to become a terrorist or get picked up by the Board of Mental Health and thrown in a white and blue room and tossed to the streets again like during the Reagan years. I suddenly realized it was my responsibility to save this poor hapless, helpless, lost lamb. I ran north like the devil along the sleek silver rails under the velvet violet night. I didn't need Apricot for my own, I was on a mission. I must save the world — heal his psychotic fears, his latent escapism which in turn would become manifest hostility or perhaps violent demonstration. It was not Apricot, not myself I ran for, it was for the women and children of America. It was for all of the helpless American goldfish, hot dogs, innocent apple pies.

Eventually after minutes of running, minutes of bitching, minutes of using every reversive inversive subversive psychology ever half-learned in public school, I caught up with Apricot and tackled him. We fell hard on the dirt and wood plank. But Apricot didn't struggle. I had him in a figure-four lock within seconds.

After an exceptionally pregnant moment, he squealed and sputtered and twisted his head painfully towards me. He had virtually no expression on his face, perhaps he was now entering acute depression. He barely moved, he seemed passive and despondent. In the dim of the night, his partial face appeared grave, stoic, and stone as that of the Moai, strewn 100s of them haphazard across the lava-riddled, fertile little Pacific navel called Easter Island. And like the Moai, he did not move, did not flinch, a million ancient lost years of a second, a million arcane human scenarios whirred psychedelically by, a million ancient promises held up to the heavens in slow-to-change rock — bracing their hard gravel obelisk fists to nature and modern civilization. That's what the look on Apricot's face said to me.

"Michelle, Michelle Domingue."

His scornful voice brought me back to the L.A. railroad yard.

"Michelle, why must you always be in control? Why must you always be on top?"

I let go of him.

"Whadda ya want? Hmm? Whadda ya want from me?"

I didn't know what to say, his question out of the blue like that struck me dumbfounded.

"If it's the book. If it's the sex scenes in the book, the lies, the stretches of the imagination, the exploitation of our profound connection, the capitalization of your now legendary name, the things I made you say in the book which you never said, the fact that my book outgrossed your verbal exploits monetarily in the past 24 hours, the fact that I'm going to win a Nobel Prize this year and you are not, and that bananas are out of season in Bulgaria this time of year. Well all I can offer is my apologies and a sock."

Yes, a sock. He pulled off the brown Fruit of the Loom stocking, an offering, a humble sacrifice in the face of major injustice. I took it and threw it out there, out somewhere in the dark, somewhere in the abyss, the Los Angeles void.

"There are two things I ask of you, Michelle Domingue. One, that you never criticize my theory of compensation. It is still but a child and needs love and nurturing in order to grow into a full-fledged scientific law. And secondly, that you just shut up with all this bullshit chit chatter tickety talk and move us on to the next scenario. Take me, Michelle, take me away, say something my love and get me outta this sooty gravel-gutted train yard. Take me and my mind away the way you can. With your way, with your words. Verbatize me."

Deep black. Silence. Empty. My back cracked as I heaved out a breath of historical dark moss-covered Michelle Domingue conscious think. Deeply I flew past Egypt, past Sumer, past Plato's Atlantis. Then in a sudden beauty of an instant I was back touching Apricot in the train yard.

YOU'VE COME INTO YOUR OWN. NOW YOU'VE GOTTA CLEAN IT UP.

Apricot leaned over, kissed me right on the eyebrow with puffy tender lips, leaned back and smiled.

"So true, Michelle Domingue, surely you are a Christ of your own time."

I , needless to say, blushed and accepted the compliment as best I could.

From a short distance away we saw it heaving forward, churning and vibrating its way our direction, a white beacon of warning pulling a mighty hulk of long dark metal. Chunk a chunk a metal. It was chunka chunka slower and slower, it was the 11:15 for Fresno. I hope I get some raisins in Fresno. I looked at Apricot, Apricot looked at me. Would it be? Would it be Fresno? Or would we could we in a car or follow a star? Was it to be Fresno or the romantic pull of Peru — Machu Picchu, Cuzco? Something in me said, "Hell, Michelle, maybe this time Dad will pay." Something else in me said, "I'm something in you and I want out." Something else said, "Do it till you're satisfied, whatever it is." Me and Apricot were just looking, staring, thinking, like that for about twenty seconds till we joined fingers, and walked toward the brilliant and still stream of train light, feeling human and undecided.

Somewhere in my 25 hard-bitten years of life experience, I learned that if one is to be heralded, exalted in any form, one must do one of two things. A: shun that which is bestowed upon you. Search only for an inner truth no matter what temptation capitalism may offer. Or B: Do as the post-hippie naturalists do and "go with the flow." Within those two philosophies, the round hole thought and the square hole thought, I, Michelle Domingue, a seven-sided peg, made the Almighty attempt to fit. In the hours that passed, the hours since the Media uncovered and exploited my unusual and do I dare say miraculous? gift of word, I was bestowed, by public and private audience, hundreds and hundreds of dollars. The question of what to do with all this cash of course became the mainstay of conversation between Apricot and myself—breakfast, lunch and dinner while basking in the hot muggy San Joaquin Valley. The money came to me by wire, Apricot and I had boxcar-hitched onto the old 11:15 up to Fresno, but landed in Delano, a midsize grape town smack dab in the middle of flatness, between

Bakersfield and Fresno. We stayed at the Starlight Lanes Motel, bowled till dawn and then sunk in our wonderful starchy stiff white motel bedsheets, falling asleep to "Stardust" on the local morning radio. Just before dawn, just before sleep, just before the magic morning light could blot it away, the little Delano Airport talked to me. Playing patterns on our motel wall, it turned its green and white lights round and round, lulling me into a hypnotic and best-ever sleep.

But sleep would only serve to delay the decision. Not only did I, Michelle Domingue, have the sudden appearance of hundreds of dollars, but some time before that astounding week was out, Apricot would be recouping royalties off his marginally factual account of our love story, *In and Out of Bed with Michelle Domingue*. We were guaranteed thousands there. So what does one do with all this cash? Apricot tossed around the idea of buying into Gucci's or I Magnin's or some such thing. I thought about hot air balloons and buying into favorite political campaigns. But what finally came to pass was far more interesting, less expensive, more spontaneous, and promised to put me a little less in the limelight.

We needed a vacation. I needed time. I had powerful books to devour. Deep philosophical and spiritual research to develop. Then there was Apricot with his precious theories of compensation.

Yes, time. We needed time to postulate and conceptualize. And we needed a land where we could do all this. Something foreign, deep, mysterious and romantic. A place where we could be alone.

I found the library and the travel services had just the answer. In no time at all I had a shopping cart full of travel books and brochures concerning every exotic corner of the world. Apricot and I could plop down in one nice little faraway wonderland like Pompeii, Italy or Budapest, Hungary, or do a travel jaunt through several countries. One brochure pointed out how we could do Homer's route: Greece, Crete, and various other parts of Odysseus's Mediterranean. Another travel booklet sold us on ideas of following the Jews' & Moses' footsteps from Egypt to the Promised Land. Though even with discretion and budgeting, treks of this sort can prove disastrous. The tour that looked the most appetizing was a journey from the Mesopotamian outskirts to Lhasa in the Tibetan Himalayas. The purported journey Jesus made in those "missing" years to study glacial disintegration or some such thing with the Dalai Lama.

After much talk, a decision was finally reached. Apricot was to take himself and his growing theories into Big Bear (snow and sun wonderland of SoCal) and I to to New York City. It was only at the last minute during an intense purge of my own soul/mind that I came to realize the call New York was putting forth to me, Michelle Domingue. Oh sure, I'd received the thousands of letters pleading for my arrival, my touch, my face, my healing powers, my clothes, my cosmetic line, my my my, so much. It came as inspirations so often do for me, in a flash, a thunderous clap of a moment vivid yet vague, solid yet nebulous, hard yet flaccid, all one figure-eight march of Godliness. With Prof. Harold Hill pumping the baton at the forefront, a huge procession, a Macy's parade, a child crusade, stamping and stepping high to my drum. Yes, I, Michelle Domingue, was to go to New York City and heal and learn and rest. How? Incognito. The plan streamed through my mind for a brief brilliant moment. Yes, yes! Each day a new identity, each day a new scenario. A mastermind of an idea! God and I were brainstorming. The vast nothing void vowed to lay down opportunity in my lap. I knew that I, Michelle Domingue, could achieve my goals and get in anywhere at any time, if only by sheer charisma and good cosmetics, and I wanted New York, that is to say I wanted to heal New York. The letters that its twelve million citizens had been scratching out and mailing to me were heart-rending. My mission lay before me. Like leaves on a lawn, like lovers hand in hand, like clouds in the sky, like the moon in the night, like sand on the shore, like water down a gutter, my mission lay before me.

Dear Michelle Domingue,

Hope you can come out, stay for supper, stay the night, go to Coney Island.

Love, Aunt May

Dear Michelle,

I read your biography *In and Out of Bed* and you really turn me on BAD. I need you out here in Brooklyn, you sexy thing. Also, could you send a pubic hair through the mail? I'll treasure it forever, sweets.

Vinnie

P.S. Gang wars killed my whole family, write soon.

Dear Mish,

Please send an autographed 8 by 10 of you healing the masses.

Love, Richard

Dear Miss Domingue,

Looking forward to your hoped-for arrival in the Apple. Preparations for the interview and pix can be set within a moment's notice. This could be our biggest seller since Madonna. Numerous fab pix ideas: 1. Michelle Domingue naked breaking a penis-shaped bread with male apostle-looking onlookers/Last Supper overtones. 2. Michelle Domingue naked and nailed to a cross. 3. Michelle Domingue naked with scantily clad Mary Magdalene-type woman. 4. Michelle Domingue in gauze shroud with beads and flowers sitting on the very *peak* of a Himalayan mountaintop. 5. Michelle Domingue fully clothed feeding poison to a captive, naked, and devout following. 6. Well, the list goes on. Contact me for more details. Looking forward to doing business.

Love ya babe, Bob G.

P.S. I've got a little bowel problem that could use some healing.

Dear Michelle Domingue,

This is my 50th letter to you, my 50th plea, my love for you is clear, pure and deep. I can't live without you. Come to me my darling, heal me, need me, touch me feel me. If you do not come to me I will have to kill you then my pet rat Phillip then myself. God would not like this therefore you must arrive promptly. Also, if you come see me you can heal my psychosis so get here quick you knucklehead.

Love, Ralph

Dear Miss Michelle Domingue,

Hi, I'm with the Long Island edition of *The New York Times*. Just writing to let you know we do have delivery in your area each day before six a.m. and would like to get the paper delivered to you. Also we do give over $150.00 worth of food coupons away weekly, so the paper essentially pays for itself. Give us a try.

Thanx, Debbie
New York Times Field Representative

Dearest Michelle Venus,

What's this I hear 'bout you being a big time Christ, for Chrissakes? I 'member you as a bratty little tike with fat puffy pinchable cheeks. What kinda publicity stunt you doin'? Me and your Aunty Rosie read 'bout you in the *Star*, see you embarrassing your papa like that. Your auntie and I barely go out any more—people, our very own neighbors all our lives here in Levittown, are looking funny at us now. How would you feel if your little cutie "normal as a child" niece became a son of God? Now, not only have we got the police, FBI, and IRS watching us, but God too. Because of your little Messiah phase, I can't drink, Auntie can't bet at bridge, your cousin Walter can't fornicate with his girlfriend. We were a happy little normal Levittown USA family — till your hobby became a habit. When are you going to settle down anyway, get a real job? Both your father and I know this is just another phase. And are you seeing any nice young men? This book this Mr. Apricot wrote on you was enough to run us outta town, the very nerve of the young man! You're always dating the wrong types, always the bad side of the tracks, always a no-'count, always a penniless hippie bum! You're worth better, Dear. Does God have any intention of marrying you and Jesus? Your Auntie and I think you would make the loveliest couple. Anyway, why didn't he pick a girl named Mary?— the Church still doesn't understand that; why he picked a "Michelle-Venus." Michelle, your papa said you've been dealing with a vitamin deficiency lately and this has been affecting your health. You be sure to call on us once you come out east. Your Auntie Rosie will fix you up with a good healthy meat and potatoes meal — fix you right up. Take care sweetheart.

Your Uncle Leo

P.S. write soon, my little battleaxe

And even as this fate-rendered mission lay clearly before me, Michelle Domingue, so too did the body of my own Apricot. I can still to this day remember the heartwrenching decision we preoccupied ourselves with. Do we stay together in all our loving glory, or strike out on our own in the cold cruel world of individualism? Could I really make myself get on that plane and fly across the hunk of dirt called U.S.A. to a nether world away from my true soul mate "Ape"? I remember curling up next to him in our little motel room bed with our clothes fully on because we had decided only hours before we would no longer consummate our relationship until marriage vows were exchanged — clothes and separate bedsheets would suffice. I was dead set on a white lace wedding and returning to God-touched virginity. Anyhow, back to my agony. The sun shone splendidly through the window as Apricot and I lay hand in hand eye to eye thought to thought.

"Oh baby why do you want to go up to that Godforsaken smog-laden ski lodge? It's stupid, I tell you. Oh come with me. my darling."

"You know I can't, my Michelle, not now, not in the midst of my wildest brainstorm of ingenious creativity, not in the midst of the final chapters to my theories of compensation."

"But Darling, I don't care about your theories of compensation. I don't understand them, the average Broadway or Macy's shopper would never understand them."

"But scientists do, sweets."

"Who cares about stupid scientists? If you want to give them something, give them an eye or a leg, it's so much less confusing than your theories, and besides...I love you...don't you see that, can't you read it in my eyes, smell it, feel it in my touch?"

"Oh dearest Michelle, yes, yes. And yet at times no, no, I don't. At times you belong to no one, not even yourself, you belong to God and the world and perhaps you will one day leave me for that guy Jesus..."

"Oh stop it, I'm just sick of that, ever since that letter from my uncle, don't you dare assume. They're just trying to fix me up, you know. Just don't talk like that."

"...and I get jealous of God, Michelle babe, I mean in the past 48 hours you've spent more time with God than with me, and it just isn't right for a young girl to go traipsing off, when I'm your regular suitor. I love you, Michelle Domingue, but I don't think you are ready for a real commitment. Perhaps once you go to New York City and sow your oats and heal your crowds and mingle with the wealthy, you can then decide."

"Apricot, love, what are you saying?"

"Just that I don't need a messiah, Michelle Domingue, I need a woman. Simple."

"Is it, is it, what is it?"

"That, is it."

"What if..."

"What if, smut if, we need a separation, and that's that. Of course...I'll still love you..."

Mr. Apricot was, of course, right, damn him. And within moments he was packed and marching himself out the door, knit snow-cap and all. He seemed so happy about the whole thing, even a little smug. Hmph, who cares? Michelle Domingue has got the masses, she's got New York, she's got a recording contract with Sony Records pending, she's got a lucky star... A lucky star, didn't Apricot say that once... "something something na na...-ar, I think I've found my lucky star"? Yes, he did.

Chapter Three

New York is grand in the fall, leaves all changing colors, the stars that you *can* see past the colossal scraper columns stand out sharp and pointed. The smell of urine is not quite so stingingly pungent as in the sweaty summers. Yet year around some trace of human piddle is wafting about as a constant reminder that men like to show their wares, particularly in Manhattan downtown parks and subways. It's a funny thing—and yet so human, so male—and so New York, I don't remember much of that in Los Angeles. Nonetheless I was ready for it, the urine, the cold and breezy Eastern winds in preparation for snow and the turn of leaves and the frozen brown grasses. And the old cobblestone throughways trodden by many Americans for the last 200 and some odd years or I suppose even longer, and at last yes ready for the warm welcome by the wanting masses and media.

God only knew how long I'd stay, when one is a messiah one does not ask such fleshly and earthen questions, one waits for signs. And the sign had been given by the tower to the plane and we were rising, as I pondered on life and God, and I was spiritually rising as well. The whoops of the stomach took us deep into God's golden sky, piercing the pompon clouds and rising into a lighter whiter sky. I, Michelle Domingue, read Plato, contemplated potatoes, looked out the window. Note: a question has arisen in my mind...why do I become more spiritually sensitive in the wake of fear or disaster?

The plane ride was quite lovely, quite cheap with exceptionally tasty meals: I had the kosher special. I won't go into detail, a plane ride is a plane ride, we all deal with the fears: the instant replays of the shuttle disaster of '86, the gritting teeth, the desperate eye searches for the flight attendants, watching their eyes their smiles the wrinkles in the brow, the meter of their speech, the constant growl of a working engine, the delicacies of tone in the captain's address. But a flight is a flight, and it landed, and Michelle Domingue was safe and sound in Newark Airport.

There was a pleasant yet unassuming entourage waiting for me on the Newark Airport grounds. Some of my fans had come together for the day, displaying banners and ribbons and buttons and gone in on supplying us with a big old school bus to transport me into Manhattan. They were an unexceptional but humble bunch, mostly housewives taking the day off. Heard of my intended arrival on this week's news. The school bus was in actuality a ridiculous gesture on their part, but how were they to know I was disgusted by the smell of old vinyl? Nonetheless I smiled thankfully while Greta, a large 40-year-old mother of three, escorted me and my baggage into the old jalopy. And we were off. The modest-sized bus crowd, having enclosed me, ballyhooed at my arrival in that high-pitch yowl that women often make when excited. It was piercing and quite loud. "Speech, speech!" they cried. Even if I'd had a damn thing to say, even if I could have moved my stiff-from-quickened-emotion mouth, even if I could've, not a thing could be heard. So I sunk into my lungs a deep collective breath/thought and breathlessly mimed in the highest of artistic fashion a brilliant if nonexistent speech. The bus continued to screech through the various labyrinths of airport roads, the women wheezed, whooped and jangled their jewelry. The old men clanked canes to bus metal and whirred party noisemakers. After nearly fifteen minutes of ongoing farce, the crew became tired. So did I, with a very deliberate closing-of-the-mouth finality, arms gesticulating to finish the pantomime (i.e. my poignant oratory). I'd cleverly managed to outwit the witless crowd, the more they'd cheer the more I'd mime. After some time I'd tired of the charade and sat myself humbly amidst a flurry of confetti and (in general) flabby handshakes. God knows

I was not born for this. I, Michelle Domingue, was not born for politics. No, I am just a mere subject of the holy muse. A simple servant to the will of an unseen God. And so I'd had my fun, and when fun is completed it indeed is done. I let myself into a trance-like sleep and did not awaken until the clank clatter honk of midtown Manhattan.

It quickly became quite evident that we would not make our destination. The Waldorf Astoria, Cadillac of Hotels, was deluged with admirers and apparent saint-seekers. The bus and its loadful hung still in the thick of traffic and mankind mania. Many of the people clutched the day's edition of the *New York Post*, which boasted a very attractive photo of me with the headline "Midtown Messiah!" A hush came over the jalopy, the growling man of a bus driver was shouting something. "Ain't going, ain't going into that. We're turning around." It was quickly decided by my huddled entourage that the best way to camouflage a messiah was to veil her with the mask of the everyman. The quaint and quiet Washington Square Hotel was decided upon, an old inn on the edge of Washington Square park.

It was a good safe choice, we arrived practically unnoticed. A civilian did notice the lovely fabric of my sporting attire and commended me for it. Other than this brief contact, I was nearly invisible. Twelve of my friends checked me into the modest if dingy room and, fearing for my safety, changed their home commitments and checked themselves in as well. We all agreed to dinner and conversation at the pizza cafe on the corner. In the meantime, I took restful refuge in the smallness of my room. The one light on the ceiling was evidently out, and so I turned the TV on as a visual aid. The news is on in New York 24 hours a day. The sound was off, and I lay on the quicksand of a bed and reflected quietly. What could I, Michelle Domingue, possibly give to these many many people? These hungry faces. Oh God, am I merely a buffoonery in a beautiful dress?

The bathroom faucet seemed to be tapping out a scrambled answer to me. It tapped and it tapped and into that sound, that persistent, measured drip-drip, I did fall. It seemed my whole self was being sucked into a whirlwind of some kind. My body surely was not moving, yet my mind was somehow reeling, pulled further into the realm of that tap-tapping. Then it all stopped. In the darkness of my room I could barely make out the wallpaper mural behind the staticky TV set. It was a painting of an alder tree. Without a rational thought in my head I walked to it and instinctively snapped off a twig. I was suddenly surprised to find an oak and beech twig also in hand. Was this sort of conjuring a fringe benefit for a messiah?

The blue TV fire flickered as I held this mystery trinity. A great welling-up of good cheer came over me, a summons of universal wisdoms. A thrilling eddy of stars overtook me. I was aware of standing still and a great racing of movement at once. Suddenly a ripe fruit came into view. The musty motel room faded. The fruit grew in stature and hovered with an eerie glow. Somehow, I was not afraid. I was still aware of clutching the trinity of twigs — so long as I held onto my treasure, I would be immune from wrong, safe. The large round fruit pulsated, I could not yet make out its genus. Then the twigs began to rumble lightly in my grip. The beech became a snake, the oak a dog, and the alder a crow. I have no idea how they got there, dear readers, but they seemed quite comfortable in my palm. The dog was white and wore a pair of Joycean eyeglasses. He addressed me first:

"Michelle, Michelle, your visions tell of a secret in hiding in your wishing well."

Well, that of course being gobbledygook to me, I retorted with a humph! from the most holy of places.

"Yes, yes," spoke up the crow, his wings made of pure and solid gold.

"Yes, yes," he repeated emphatically.

"Is that a truth?" I asked.

"Yes and yes," he laughed out again.

"Well go on and take up what's yours," said the snake.

"My eyes have gone bad from all my reading."

"But take up this treasure that has been bestowed on you from on high." The snake sounded like a crotchety old man, the type that I, Michelle Domingue, annoyed as a child.

("Get off this yard you children.")

But the snake had little more to say. The golden-winged crow punctuated the conference with yes-yeses. Then as quickly as they had arrived they departed. And with a coming together of their noses they vanished in a blink of white light. All that was left of their legacy was an apricot in hand and an odd desire to scribble onto hotel stationery. This I did and this is what it read:

THE SEVEN MEN OF ASPARAGUS
COULDN'T GET DOWN THEIR
ESOPHAGUS.
I FOUND OUT LATER, WHEN HE LOST
HIS FLAVOR
HE WAS WIDE AS A BLACK
RHINOCEROS.

Then the flicker-blue of familiar newstime TV returned. Had I been sleeping, dreaming? This was some kinda vision to be sure. I would save the apricot mystery and the obvious reflections on my own Mr. Apricot for a later hour, another time. Ah time, it had slipped from my grasp. I had missed my pizza date, and only hoped my good followers would forgive me. Somehow, some way, hours had bustled by in the blink of a TV blue eye.

New York swells up around you like a huge phallus. When you're in the mood, there's no one quite like him, nobody does it better. The lights. The night action, the constant hustle, the hot dogs and pizza, the small businesses with great food and homemade merchandise, oh and the art! Fifth Avenue department stores, quick commuter jumps to the Hamptons, the snow on top of cars! The bumpy speedy taxis that invariably have no shocks. Mr. Toad's Wild Ride, indeed!

Oh New York. Old New York. Owe New York. You don't wanna.

I'd only brought along one little ol' credit card to New York City. But I promised myself I simply would not use it. Not even once. That was out! And then I realized, Geeze, I'd only allowed myself $300.00 worth of traveler's checks.

And so the New York winds began to blow. I was on Astor near St. Marks, the place they call "the cube." A small island between streets, home of a fairly obtrusive metallic cube/art. It made me think of of mankind's struggle against the boxes of life. This cube, cold and metallic, would be so much warmer and symbolic in L.A., for in the city of Angels life is but a box. Each morning you get off of your box spring, go to the box shower, to box car, to box office, to box lunch, to box car, to box home, to television, to box spring. The complete box cycle.

And what was I to do at 4:00 in the afternoon in New York City with a mere $300 in my pocket? Ah, but go to the p.o. box Apricot had set up for me, and check my fan mail. If there's one thing that will brighten up a seemingly sour day for a two-day-old messiah, it's fan mail.

I rushed, ran, very quickly, for I was quite depressed, to my post office on 14th between A and First. I followed his instructions, make a right, get key from clerk, Box #2753. I was shaking, tears were beginning to well up, the damn key! The goddamn key wouldn't work. I took deep slow breaths, relax, breathe. I told myself to calm down. Myself said no. It was sad and didn't know why. I said, listen myself you've got to take it easy, you're all right you know, it's just a shock and all, being in such a new place, New York. You'll feel better once you get a bit to eat. It'll be all right. Myself kept shaking, but my soothing voice had calmed it to the point of realizing it had been forcing, jabbing, punching in Dad's house key. Still, slightly trembling, it pushed in the correct key and pulled the small door out. A continual stream of white cascaded upon us for almost a minute. I was nearly overwhelmed. I stopped shaking. I was happy. There must be one hundred and fifty-seven letters here. I was happy, but I wasn't surprised. A two-day old messiah learns to live with adoration, takes it in stride, in fact comes to expect adoration.

An old Jewish woman walked by. She had a wiry frame and a crooked gait. "And who are you? Santa Claus?" I smiled in a patronizing sort of way.

"You'd think my son would write. But does he? No."

She had very thick glasses on and didn't recognize me, the famous Michelle Domingue.

"You'd think he wouldn't move away, but there he goes to California to be a hippie bum in cowboy boots!" She was waving the evening paper in meter with her chatter. "He's a cantor and belongs in synagogue, he should be at his studies and singing like a bird, like a cantor can sing in synagogue."

I was picking up my letters and half listening, half floating thoughtless, when I began noticing her staring at me good and thorough.

"My Joshua left his good mother, left the only father that loved him, and put on hippie boots in California. New York City isn't good enough. No, he wants to run around the country with a psycho woman, thinks she's God, thinks she's Jesus H. Christ." She huffed an ironical breath, then started back up. "We saw them in the newspaper, you know, miss. And she looks a good bit like you, if I do say so." She paused and quieted herself. She was wondering what to do, I was working fast as a computer whirr picking up my scattered fan mail. The old crooked Jewish woman did slightly resemble my Apricot. Of course if it were so, I would never let on.

I continued my laboring over the mail. Fortunately, I'd brought along a Hefty trash bag, pulled it out of my purse and began stuffing. I was quite involved, and though she was a potential mother-in-law I really had nothing to say to her. Besides, I was absorbed. My people called.

I let her stare good at me another few moments and walked out of the post office without a bit of guilt. She just didn't figure into the story and well enough I'd let her go. Perhaps her story could fit into my sequel autobiography. Where I settle down with four children and Apricot and the woods. Besides, I had a destiny with the New York streets. Go forth into the place of the people, and indeed I was to.

Chapter Four

I really didn't know which way to go nor which way to turn. These things I did know: 1. No hotels. I needed to force myself out into the place of the people. 2. No money. I needed to live and breathe with the working and poverty classes. 3. I either needed to get a job or have someone supply me meager amounts of food. 4. Bathroom. I needed access to a good sit-down toilet. 5. I needed to find a good touch-tone phone to call Apricot on my MCI card (since I wasn't allowing myself a cellular). I suppose these were the main points. Now, with these in mind, I could create an opening for the perfect right experiences. And right off, I was offered numerous job positions. In Washington Square park I could sell marijuana. On Avenue B I could shine shoes. In the Village I could sell McDonalds burgers. What would I do? I was walking down Second Avenue that evening trying to decide which of these jobs could work me up the spiritual ladder. I was in a quandary. Also, I didn't want to hurt anyone and I was mildly concerned as to whether my messianic mission would conflict too much with a drug pushing day job. Was it actually any worse than working behind a computer for Convair, building bombs? My mind was whirring, my stomach growling, for I hadn't eaten in some time. I suppose I was on the corner of Second Ave. and 10th Street when I noticed a nice expensive Cadillac pulling up beside me. There was a man in the driver's seat, he was alone, staring at me. I thought truly nothing of it—he merely an admirer, one of many. I walked on. He got a green light and pulled his car up next to me again, this time motioning me to come on over. Oh there's always time in a saint's busy schedule.

"Yes," I said.

"Well, come on, girl, get in...what do you want?" he asked.

"Well, if you're buyin', I suppose a coupla slices and a cherry Coke at St. Marks Pizza."

"Is that it, girl?..."

"Well, I'd also like a lift to St. Marks Books." I needed to pick up a fresh copy of Camus' *The Stranger* and *The Mahabharata*.

"Is the car all right then?..." he asked, impatient.

"Oh sure, your car's fine, it's a real nice car, I like new ones, though I'm not particularly interested in one for myself..."

"Well, that's good," he laughed.

"Oh yes, it's a fine car. Why? Do you have doubts about this car yourself?"

"Oh," he smiled, "I just wasn't sure if it'd be, you know, comfortable for you."

He started the car moving, we were on our way to St. Marks Place.

"You're not a bad-looking girl," he said.

"Thanks, I feel quite beautiful most of the time, I use Oil of Olay, you know, the beauty cleanser and all."

"Hmmmm...you really should get a new dress if you want to do this right, it would help you in your line of work."

I considered what he was saying. Yes, perhaps my single dress wardrobe was too Los Angeles. He had a valid point.

"You could possibly be right. Maybe we should stop. Yes. Here! Let's stop here, look at that dress! The one in the window. It's me, don't you think?"

He laughed, but I could tell he wasn't laughing at me, not in that '50s Fred MacMurray sort of way, more in the new confused male role sort of way.

"Do you think you would work better in that dress?"

"Oh, yeah, yeah I would, you'll notice right off."

"Well, that's what I would expect."

I was excited, so was he, it seemed. Geeze, I thought, I'd have to be careful here, I didn't want this nice gentleman to fall in love with me.

No, no, I was spoken for. However, he was not a bad-looking man. Early forties, dark brown hair, New York Italian, what a cute accent he had, tight little butt that pouched out just right, and enough hair on his arm to cover his balding head. (He had some style, though, probably derived from handling rolls of money.) Perhaps he could endorse my Christ career so I wouldn't have to get a daytime pusher job. Things were looking up.

"This dress fits great, oh wow, I'm really thrilled. Could we go get pizza now...oh what's your name, anyway?" He was hesitant at first, then blurted it out in such a way, hoping I might not catch it. I caught it. It was Bob.

Pizza at St. Marks is almost always good, almost always a safe pick. We ate and fanned ourselves with ½ price discount handbills left on the tables. I had a cherry Coke and Bob had a classic Coke. We walked to St. Marks Books. The night was falling down on us like Connecticut leaves in autumn. It was growing pretty dark on St. Marks Place and the local hair-color parades were coming out to mingle and mix. A dog on a leash lost from its master ran up to Bob and wound his leather choke strap around Bob's leg. The dog was a mutt mix, but he liked Bob. I thought that was a good sign — dogs have an instinct for picking nice people. Bob smiled, I hadn't noticed what a nice smile he had, it made me forget his baldness. I'd never kissed a bald man, I thought, then after I thought that I immediately felt guilty—already I had made my first step toward betrayal. Already I'd ruined my love for Apricot, poor precious Apricot. Geeze, I'd already forgotten how Apricot smelled. I'd forgotten about his tightly trimmed sideburns, his funny-lookin' little toe, the way he could make me so mad by the use of his cockeyed brilliance, his smell...how was it? Sweet? What did apricots smell like? Bob and I passed by a Vietnamese-owned vegetable stand. I made a quick passing inspection, they did not sell apricots. Maybe N.Y.C. didn't have apricots. I felt sorta, a little bit, sad.

I slept on a park bench that night. I had the bald man drop me at the St. Mark's Church. I wouldn't even let him kiss me goodnight. He looked mad about that. He said he expected a full night of sex for the new dress. I told him that was impossible. Then he got this funny look in his eye, a scared glint. The bald man said "Get out," he practically threw me out, saying, "Get out, get out, you homo!" He thought I was a man.

I shared the park bench in front of St. Mark's Church with a mumbling brown paper bag of a man. He had one half of the bench, I had the other, I made sure his feet never touched mine. The brown hair ball of a man left before sunrise, his bottle had fallen through the bench slats and woken us both with its apocalyptic alarm clock clatter. The brown hump heaved himself forward, his old black work-men's shoes scraping and scuffing over the cobble-stone walkway. They say you lead first with the part of your body you're most confident of. This brown clump lead with his head, the top of his grizzly bear hair. It pointed like a seaman's compass due north. He moved as though pulled along by an invisible thread down Second Avenue toward the soon-coming vitamin-D sun. We are all attracted to the light. But I was tired and wanted to soak a while longer in the nothingness limbo of sleep.

I awoke again, this time the sun was up. I remember I'd been dreaming. I'd been dreaming of Apricot. Where oh where was he now, where was that brilliant mind of his taking him? What visions, theories, equations, to what exponential power, was he dreaming up? A light wind kicked up and brushed the trees above me. The leaves whispered nagging secrets to one another. "Her Apricot has got his mind on other, more worldly women." "Such a shame." "She left him, thought she was too good," "My my." "Good corn weather, ain't it?" "She thinks she's doing this world some good, only good would be goin' back to her loved ones." "That poor, poor man," "That poor Mr. Apricot had to follow his manly whims, any man would." "Mm hmm." Crooked twigs wagged their fingers at me. The leaves shook their heads. The oak bent his heavy head while the wind moaned on my behalf. All such a shame.

But wait, could it be true? Was my Apricot pursuing his masculine ways? Oh damn, why couldn't I be a normal woman, a housewife, an unwed mother, a secretary? I drew in a long deep breath. I needed some comfort. And where were my visions of late anyway, where were my messianic messages? Oh Father on high, whaddup? Was this worth it, the self-inflicted poverty, tearing myself away from the comforts of California, my wealthy upbringing, my love—oh my love, Apricot. The early morning sun still too weak to warm the city cement, I squeezed myself tighter against the mid-autumn breeze. The city of New York was slowly thawing, within an hour the six-seven cars in front of me would multiply exponentially. I yearned for my childhood. Maybe I could have been the angel my father wanted. God knows I tried. Ballet looked like an untailored suit on me. Horses, I was afraid of them and had sold my first horse, secretly for glue. A blue-grey gelding — what did he have to look forward to in life anyway? — 1000 bales of hay, some oats, people bouncing around on his back, a salt lick, forget the mares, forget the wild fields, it's a ten by ten stall for you. No, I couldn't bear it, forgive me Snookers. Oh Father! I never pleased you. Perhaps now, when you see my name in a headline or my face on *Time* Magazine and see that others love and respect me, you too will feel something other than repulsion, something...good, at the sight or the sound of Michelle Domingue. I think I must love you, Father.

I was aroused by temptation that morning in front of the stone majesty of St. Mark's Church. The temptation to use one of my traveler's checks. Yes, the money had been sent by admiring fans sponsoring my spiritual searchings. Yet I'd promised myself and God that I would go without. Let nature provide. The temptation flared and flamed, and danced tricks in the morning light. It masqueraded as strolling yuppies munching croissant sandwiches. It pretended to be businessmen with steaming bags of fresh egg bagels. It all came together and culminated in the head of me, Michelle Domingue, hungry on a park bench in downtown New York City then lasered out a shot. Boom! Crossing the street, zeroing in, targeting, yes! I ran to that spot and there it sat, a perfect apple on a perfect apple stack. I did not see the vegetable stand proprietor, my my he had such an abundance of foods. Surely he would never miss this sweet honey of an apple. I grabbed the apple quickly and clumsily and ran. Then I heard him yelling behind me, he was calling me a bum and never even saw my face. Me, Michelle Domingue, a thief! I took several bites from the luscious red fruit, chewed them, then suddenly spat them out upon the Manhattan asphalt. Poison. Poison to the spirit. There were only two small bites from the apple when I returned it to its owner. The man at the vegetable stand was not pleased with the ¾ths of an apple. He was yelling at me in some Asian language. I bowed my head, ashamed. I had picked the forbidden fruit.

"Forgive me sir, for I have sinned."

It was then that the Asian-American recognized me. It dawned on him, like the dawn.

He took my chin in his hand, softly, gently. And raised my eyes up to meet his.

"You are Ms. Michelle Domingue, Saintess. Yes?"

"Why yes, I am."

"I did not recognize you, I am so sorry. I beg your forgiveness. Have as many apples as you like."

"Thank you sir, thank you, but no, I cannot accept a prize for thievery." I fell to my knees, an honest show of saintliness. "I am afraid dear sir I am no Saint Francis. Forgive me."

And with that I took my leave. I heard him say something anxious to his wife in Vietnamese.

"Boing Boing Boing Michelle Domingue."

("She is no Saint Francis.") Dejected from my own lack of will, I wove my way back to Washington Square Hotel, thinking, walking, questioning. Perhaps the vow of poverty was not my crown. Perhaps I was just another raving heretic who must soon join the 42nd St. fold raging to the abyss on apocalyptic riddles. Ah, and so. Prophetess of impending doom. More than once I must say the face of that dear Apricot filled the screening room of my mind. A face that too often haunted me now. Ah, my beloved, thou art fair my hero.

Damn, this place was a dump. Sixty bucks a day to make the lobby look good and the room's dark and dingy —the bulb over my bed was out and the bathroom light was dim, all I had for light was the TV set. I quickly turned it on. Richard Simmons was talking about his diet plan. He had a fat person on the phone and was saying how he'd "been there." He went on and on for minutes with his story of how he'd lost weight and how he'd hated himself fat. The guy on the phone was crying. I could hear him sob between Richard's pauses. There was one good long break and the guy said, "I still don't believe it's really you—you callled me. I can't believe...."

Richard Simmons was calm, he said something thoughtful and encouraging. It made me think he really cared about this voice on the phone. I just couldn't believe he cared about this person like that. I wanted to buy the diet plan and I was six pounds underweight. I began to cry. What a stupid thing to cry about. But all that compassion and that fat guy crying on TV like that, not even caring. I wanted to slip into my bed, eat chocolates, order out for Chinese and not see the world for days. I wanted to cry a reservoir. And so it began. I turned down the sound. Richard Simmons had said good-bye to the caller and was talking more about his diet plan and how to order it. I sat there watching his hands move around the package of diet food, the black and white TV blinking in the dark small window of a room, the subliminal quake of a passing subway train. I cried a long time. Then I slept for about four hours. That kinda gentle and merciful sleep that happens. There was nothing at all left in the world except the nothing void of hotel slumber. Then a strange thing happened. There was a boom of a bang at my door—it woke me. I realized someone was knocking at my door, someone was here to see me, Michelle Domingue.

"Who is it?"

"Open the dumb door Michelle."

I couldn't believe the voice.

"It's Apricot."

Sure, it was his voice, but what the hell was he doing in New York City?

I ran to the bathroom, washed my face and patted my hair back. It was looking rather mussed. My eyes wore definite signs of turmoil. I smashed my face to a towel, rubbing color back in. Then went for the door. Oh. It was him.

"Come in," I offered.

He was looking sheepish—it scared even me, a modern messiah, if indeed I was still one.

"I'm here just briefly to see you, thanks, I'll stand at the door."

We stood and stared at each other off and on, looking at the ground, looking at the sign on the door sez do not disturb, looking at anything.

"Michelle Domingue. I'm here to tell you. Well...I'm getting married. Yes, I'm getting married. And I just wanted to tell you myself so that it wasn't some kinda shock or anything. But I'm getting married and moving from California to Long Island."

I didn't say anything. I just thought that maybe I hadn't really woken up, that this was all a weird dream.

"See, she lives on Long Island, and we'll be moving there and I have some money now from those book sales, see. And I'm trying to simplify my life, see. Besides I'm doing so well with my scientific studies that, uh, the Navy just hired me for some project they've got in mind, and the money's good."

He stopped talking. I didn't talk at all. I didn't even think. I think I did remember watching the Richard Simmons show earlier and recalled the way his hands moved and the sounds of the fat caller sobbing so honestly.

I did feel, though. I felt dead. I closed the door without even knowing it and turned the TV up. A Mets game. The Mets and the Dodgers were on. I don't know why I hated the Dodgers so much, no personality. I wondered if Dodgers manager Vernon Pupfish had tried the Richard Simmons diet plan. Pupfish looked so slim these last so many years. And the Mets, sentimental favorites, but they certainly weren't what they used to be.

Apricot was banging on the door calling my name, Michelle Domingue, over and over. He was saying stuff I couldn't make out, so I turned the TV volume down a bit so I could take in a little monologue.

"I still love you I just can't marry a messiah. Don't you understand? It'll always be you, Michelle. Michelle! Talk to me—let me see you. I'll always be in love with you my darling—we were the grandest of lovers. We were the grandest. Michelle, open up."

I got the basic gist of what he was saying and raging about, so I turned the game back up. The volume didn't quite blast out the Apricot noise, but it did scramble it. Now I settled back into my bed, dug through my bag and pulled out a leftover ½ of a Mars bar, chomped away at it while Eli Pinkus got two strikes then hit a mad homer out into the left field stands of Shea. Wow. Just then a funny thing happened. The overhead light bulb in the hotel room blinked back on. Wow. There was this home run and then the light, and the deep dark chocolate of a saved ½ of a Mars bar. Everything would be OK. I wondered if I was still a messiah. Then Pupfish called Christian Rosencrans up to the pitcher's mound. Did he still have the knack? It must have been around the eighth inning when the banging and yakking ceased. The noise just stopped. And I was thankful.

Chapter Five

Oh it's a brand new day yeah yeah hey hey.
I'll just grab my bags yeah and be on my way...

The president of my New York fan club, "The Apostles Association," called and woke me at 8 a.m. There was some morning show on the tube — it'd been on all night, keeping me company. I wondered what weird stuff I'd been taking in subconsciously. Somehow in the recess of my sleeping mind, I recalled "Branded" around 5:30 in the morning, "The Avengers" around 5. This was a reassuring thought, for perhaps the characters' strength and dignity on both of these old shows could pull me through a rather questioning time.

Ken Jackowitz was on the phone and wanted to know if we could meet for breakfast and work out the New York media strategy regarding my new-found popularity.

"The head office has been getting a million calls wondering when your next sermon will be and do you have a dial-a-prayer service?" "It's just crazy, Michelle Domingue, I mean I've worked for a number of celebrities organizing their tours and media conferences and never have I seen such a demand. I mean, I don't wanna say the Beatles, but the Beatles, ya know."

It was so strange. I didn't feel like being a celebrity. I'd lost the inspiration. Where oh where was my muse, where were you God when I needed you? I felt like soon enough people would see me as a fake and I too, not unlike Chuck Connors, would be "branded." It warmed my heart to know another had shared this plight.

"Ken," I jolted, bolt upright, "I'll meet you at Odessa's on A. at 9:00."

"O.K.," he said, and we clicked the line.

Now wait a minute, here, this was a brand new day wasn't it. Apricot had bid his farewell last night. The deluge of feelings had swept over even my highest mountains, and today there was the singing of birds. This! Was a new day. The TV was turned off. I grabbed my dress, washed off the soiled spots left from descent into dark park bum-ness, combed out every rat of hair, applied fresh makeup and even smiled at myself in the mirror.

"A new day for you, Michelle Domingue, now welcome to New York City."

Oh my it was lovely outside, little birdies chirping, sinsemilla-men selling and smiling. Folk singers in

Washington Square were singing a happy American song. My pace was fast and strong down St. Marks past the church. There was my old bum companion, the yang to my yin, sleeping on our old park bench, oh such were the days. I'd learned so much since then. I was growing more self-assured and confident each block I'd take. I even skipped between Avenues 2 and A while whistling "Red Red Robin" and thinking fondly of the Mitch Miller singers.

There was a teenage punk girl with her choke-chained pit bull in front of Odessa's. They were asking for money. Of course, I still had none, and so offered the grandest gift of all, a smile. She looked straight back at me into my eyes. At first her pit bull growled, then he too looked deeply at me. She was so young and fresh and beautiful, even with her scowl and dirty cheek, gosh those uninhibited eyes.

FAR AWAY IS NOT SO FAR AWAY AFTER ALL.

I said it, but didn't regret it. She smiled a million dollars back at me. Whereupon I entered the foodery and went to my breakfast.

Ken Jackowitz, President of the Apostles Association for Michelle Domingue, was already seated at a booth and carving a square-shaped bite into a waffle. It was our first meeting and so much was to be accomplished so quickly.

Ken was not a Christian. He had been raised Orthodox Jew. But his interest in Jesus and UFOs had strained him away—like wheat from a chaff—

from the rest of the fold. He'd been a fan of mine for days now and had even gone as far as writing (and publishing) a book of my known quotes with information and cross-references as to where why and when. It was a little pink book with gold lettering on the front and spine, a trade paperback of no more than 300 pages. It was called *Domingue Codex* and was sailing up the bestsellers chart. Ken gave me a promotional copy (which I still own) with a little clip off the corner to signify its promotional intent.

"Michelle, oh Michelle, this is an unprecedented visitation. Your aura is, stunning."

"Thank you Ken, I try to dress to my daily colors."

"Michelle, you are doing simply marvelously here in New York. Your book, or rather Apricot's unauthorized biography, has dominated the book charts for days, and I must say that mine is not far behind."

"Oh."

"But that is not what I am here to discuss with you, darling. I am here to present you with a proposition which was communicated to me yesterday. Darling Michelle, in a nutshell, Sony Entertainment is interested in signing and funding your missionary talks for CD and cassette. Of course they will also advance you moneys toward 'vehicular penetration of the flocks.' Michelle, it's a stupendous deal."

Ken certainly did believe it was right for me. He pulled the contract out of his coat and skidded a pen across the maple-sticky table.

"Hmm, though, do you think?..."

"Oh yes, any lawyer would approve."

So I signed right there in front of the waitress and cook. They applauded and gave me a piece of celebration cake, then all the patrons caught wind and gathered round. I sensed that, for the moment anyway, I'd done the right thing.

Ken gave me an envelope of two million dollars, and we shook hands. Everyone at Odessa's was so happy and expressive and I felt so close to them that I gave each and every one a dollar bill. A mighty cheer arose and brought gladness to my heart.

Everything was working out just fine. Now there would be no need to tap into that damnable credit card. I took it out of my purse and tore it to shreds. A plastic sacrifice! Everyone cheered, grabbed for their own plastic and tore them to bits. We all laughed and ate cake and barged out the cafe door and paraded down the street laughing and eating cake and tearing up checks, checkbooks, credit cards, and ATM cards, made our way to Tompkins Square Park and set it all aflame in a morning bum fire.

IF GO, THEN GO YOU MUST.

I said it, and those sweet patrons and two bums kissed upon my very feets while the punk rock girl smiled and Ken took pictures. How fondly I remember my first New York throng.

Ken had a tear in his eye that fell from the camera lens. He dabbed his eye with a silk sleeve from a nearby disciple, thanked him, and came over to my ear.

"Michelle, we must now depart, I am to take you to meet Jacob Blather at Sony, he's dying to meet you. Oh will he be thrilled!"

"Is he a believer of the words or the deeds?" I pondered out loud.

Ken caught sight of a cab, flagged it, and threw us into the back seat while the coffee shop patrons waved and threw rose petals.

"Michelle, Blather is completely aware of your ability, talent, and potential, I mean he is all-knowing in these ways. He signed Mary Rockett last week and the Random Houses the year before. Mary Rockett you know had that worldwide hit 'Ovarian Dreamscape' ('Oh oh Ovarian Dreamscape, you can't escape, I got you in my clutch, oh my baby prostate...')."

"Oh yeah, I remember that song!"

That song had meant a lot to me and Apricot at one time, it was *our* song. Could it only have been days before? Time was moving so quickly. So much had changed. Already "Ovarian Dreamscape" had fallen off the hit parade and Mary Rockett was a has-been. It was then I deduced that it was actually very long ago that Apricot and I had purred love words. Nothing lasts for long. How long would I, yes even I, Michelle Domingue, be of interest to a fast moving and changing world? Oh, it mattered not, God had plans for me anyways. This routine must all be part of God's plan. Did God's plan include marriage? Was I to marry God? Or Jesus? Were God and Jesus twins? Was Jesus a disguise God would put on to visit us little folks (not unlike the Roman Emperors who would cloak themselves as citizens and go listen to what the people said about their monarchy)? I knew that it would soon be time to meet the creator Itself, and God would have a lot of answering to do.

Somebody was clapping their hands in front of my face. I blinked back to reality. It was Ken. We were in the ever expanding office of Jacob Blather. There was Ken, then a desk, a chair, a sofa and far off some walls with agricultural drawings. Somewhere in there stood another figure, not Ken, not God, nor Jesus, but a man.

"Jacob, this is she, Michelle Domingue." Jacob moved toward me with a very long arm stretching even faster in my direction. The arm met me first. It appeared a nice arm with a white cuff and a great coat sleeve. There were many rings on the fingers of Jacob Blather. His face showed up next. He was balding, but had plenty of hair in the back for a tidy ponytail. A one-day beard smile. I wasn't sure yet if Jacob was a real person. I mean, there was something cardboard about him, but completely guileless. Jacob said nice things and we all sat down. When Jacob Blather touched the big chair behind his desk everything changed, he became supercharged.

"Oh, Michelle Domingue, what a true true honor to have you as a part of our family here at Sony, we are graced with your presence."

Then his phone rang.

"Excuse me," Jacob was muttering away at someone when the secretary came in and piled a stack of papers on his desk and dumped a dumpster of tapes next to the paper stack.

"You see how important Jacob is," Ken was impressing on me. "He's so busy that he doesn't even have time for you. He's just the right man for you. His busy-ness shows his competence..."

I stopped the secretary as she was dumping the last cassette tape outta the box and heading back toward the door.

"Excuse me, Ms. Secretary..."

"My name is Ursula, Ms. Domingue."

"Ursula, how do you like working here for Jacob Blather?"

"Oh honestly Michelle, he's all right. It's better than my last job as a file clerk or before that as a steak house waitress. Last week I thought I might get laid off 'cause he started seeing this twenty-year-old gal from Publicity. And you know they just make nothing over there in that department, and it seems like those women never get good promotions. So of course I was worried. But then Jenny, Jenny Bleets that's her name, came around to see Jacob the next day smashed outta her mind. She was toasted!

Drunk. Walked right into Jacob's office and started screwing around with the files, pretending like she had my job. Well that did it, of course. I kept my job and she was sent back to Publicity. They say she's the gal that helped break Mary Rockett's big song last week, and Jenny can't take the fall from grace now...but there'll be another artist another week."

Jacob threw a cassette tape at her. She dodged it and trotted out the door in a tight green skirt, waving bye-bye to us with teeter-tottering fingers. Jacob Blather was being emphatic with someone on the phone.

"Oh, I know what I said, but I would never sign that artist. It doesn't have to be rational, I'm the boss here. I just don't like his singing. No I don't have to make any sense. I don't care what I said at 10:00 this morning. Yes, I know I said I thought it would be a great idea. Now I think it's a rotten idea. I would never sign that artist. Look, I have guests, ask me again later, maybe I'll change my mind. Ciao."

"I'm sorry, where were we?"

"We were here at your desk, Jacob, sitting listening to you talk on the phone, that's where we were. Now we're here at your desk and you are not on the phone."

I think at times like this when a great koan is presented to you in the form of a simple question, you must answer unflinchingly in the form of Truth and Reality. Jacob, Ken and I were all here now sitting in a building, staring at each other with very little to say. Our presence spoke for us. We sat for maybe fifteen minutes and stared at one another, saying not a word. We could hear all kinds of things. Ursula was jabbering on the phone out the door, someone was clicking on a computer keyboard nearby, and far below Jacob's window was the sound of traffic streaming through the narrow veins of Manhattan. In a few hours the midday sun would be falling over New Jersey and I thought for a moment of my Western homeland and a great desire for raisins grew within me. Suddenly a snorkel sound came from Jacob Blather. I thought at first it was allergies, then a sob and a sniffle. Then Jacob threw his hands to his eyes and broke down weeping fiercely. Water spots appeared on the dark gray suit. Jacob put his head in his arms atop the busy desk.

"Ah ugh uh wah wah."

He was trying to communicate with Ken & me. Trying to tell us something and it must have been very important.

"Ugh, uh um wa na aah uhuh wah!" And he was then shaking his half-haired head and pounding his fist on the desk. His fist caught the edge of a CD and the CD went bouncing into the air, striking the big pile of tapes and papers that fell from their pyramid shape, skidding and bouncing onto the floor. It was awful, just a mess. Finally Jacob blurbled something intelligible.

"I, uh, I don't want this job no more, I want my Mommy! I want my M-M-Mommy! People are mad at me, always so mad, wah uh ugh ugh!"

He cried on and on blurbling about stuff, musta been half an hour. Then he thanked me, shook Ken's hand, smiled, and walked us out the door and down the hall to the drinking fountain.

"Thank you so much Michelle Domingue. I'm gonna try real hard (sniffle) to make this work good for you. I'll try to make it nice, OK? I love you like a sister now, please accept my gratitude and blessings. You, you must be a goddamn saint. "

We all had a Dixie Cup of water shared between us, and then like that we left Jacob Blather.

Chapter Six

"Oh Oh Ovarian Dreamscape you may penetrate
Into the depths of your own fate
But you can't escape Oh Oh Ovarian Dreamscape,
in my lap
You're in my trap!
I may look like an ingenue to you
And if I do that's just my ruse
Oh Oh Ovarian Dreamscape
You may think physical, but
I go mental, rape!
Oh Oh Ovarian Dreamscape if you are in my lap
You're in my trap!
Oh Oh Oh Big! Oh Oh Ovarian Dreamscape
Oh Oh Oh Big! Oh Oh Ovarian Dreamscape."

Ken had set up a big shindig show for me at
Carnegie Hall, so we took a cab there a little early
so I could relax and freshen up. My, Ken really had
everything so prepared for me. Schedules, people to

see, lectures. He was running the AAMD out of a little two-room office over the Sixth Avenue movie theater in the Village. He said there were stacks of mail to go through, hundreds of roses to smell and too many phone calls to deal with. Thus we were here hanging at Carnegie Hall with no phones and a nice cheese platter in front of us. I was maybe, perhaps, the teensiest bit concerned, for I hadn't thought of what in the world I would tell the many who would attend this evening. Then again, I never did seem to know what was gonna come outta my mouth. No doubt it would be good and helpful in some peculiar sort of way. Lights were of course very important to me. Ken made sure to have the best light show man in NYC, and I was reassured as he and his crew were piling in all assortments of floods, searchlights, spotlights, black lights, colored lights, lasers, hologrammed oddities, neons, computer-generated arrangements, etc. When people pay good money, I insist they see an amazing and professional show, and this ticket-buying audience would be paying as much as $5 to see me, Michelle Domingue.

I knew that I had to be absolutely stunning. I had noticed a little third-hand clothing shop as we parked for Carnegie, so out I went, hunting for the perfect wave. Dress, that is. Found easily enough, in the window, a gold lamé full-length gown and a lovely blonde fall to cascade down its backless depths. If only Apricot would see me in this golden get-up, he would beg to come back, messiah or not! There's no doubt that this outfit would appeal to the masses. Its appeal was so current. I mean, even though these threads and patterns were sewn upon in the '80's they appeared so current now. That could only be because real time runs about ten years behind. We may call it the '90's or the two thousand tens, but public thought always runs at least ten years behind creation. This could only be because God Hisself is so large that he does an act of creation and then it takes time for all molecules and pieces of matter to catch up with original thought and act. God is a simultaneous thought and act. Act meaning a cause or force which creates a disturbance, thus causing all else to act in due time. So in 1982 when the creator of this gold lamé dream dress first con- ceived of and assembled this idea, it took say another few months before it actually was sewn into a wear- able object, another perhaps year to make it into stores whereupon a few leaders of the packs purchased it from a $1,000 rack at Neiman-Marcus, wore it once or twice to the Grammys and then at a Hollywood party for some TV teen-star. Back in the closet not to be worn again, then! It's sold to a sec- ond- or third-hand store after eight years of inactiv- ity, whereupon I or someone of my ilk buys the piece of apparel and wears it often enough to make it a modern fad ten years after its conception.

What is it about sparkly gowns and women, anyway? I mean it's a favorite for any woman who's doin' it up right and goin' out on the town, or doin' as myself, Michelle Domingue, and standing before thousands of viewers and hundreds of lights while our dresses twinkle and flash before those exponential eyes. Certainly it is rare indeed for a man to wear glittering apparel. With the exception of some, say, provocative males.

I happen to think that women and gowns of glitter go together like the sun and the sea, like the mystery of a deep dark moonless night over a northern California vineyard.

In the afternoon off of the Santa Monica Pier, the far-reaching ocean undulates and shimmies in its blue sequins gown for the dazzled and dazzling sun. Mr. Fireball finally succumbs to her womanly wiles and falls red-faced into her arms at the end of each day, and then at night out she comes in a midnight blue sheath with silver sequins and spangles and a milky sash that sweeps around the shoulder, crosses her breast and meets at the hip. Light filmy wear for the summer nights. We women know just what a gorgeous gown can do!

Basically, essentially, in a nutshell, the Carnegie show came off without a hitch. People were cheering so loudly I have no idea what I said and even if I did indeed say something. For what I remember most was this overwhelming light show creating a wonderfully amazing atmospheric disturbance about me. Somehow, it was all so very profound, and with the lights bouncing off the glory of my golden gown I had the feeling of myself beaming/projecting a thousand places at once, thousands of points of light, reminiscent of the astonishing bombing-of-Baghdad video. I felt as though I were breaking apart into many, too many pieces. I knew I was being pulled apart by the wants and needs of each and every individual in the hall. A molecular tug o' war. Was this God's intention for me? Utter dissolution? No, I thought not. No, to dissipate into the tiny world of almost void, to live and be conscious in that strange and quiet but fast-moving realm of the sub-atomic was of little or no, interest to me, Michelle Domingue. Some are detail people, I knew that I, Michelle Domingue, was not—I was for the larger, grander view, the Great Overview. If I could, I would be a giant before I would be an ant.

"Michelle Michelle Domingue, oh we love you
Michelle Michelle Domingue, oh yes we truly do."

A sing-song chant that snapped me back, away from entropy — pulled my molecular makeup back in, cinch tight. I felt myself again, I came back into my bag of skin and of course the dress fit so well.

"Yes yes I do love you too. Though perhaps I am not completely *aware* of my love for you, I know it must be so. Because here I am in front of your adoring faces.

"Yes, I often wonder, just like you, not unlike yourselves, what is my mission here on planet Earth? What, Michelle Domingue, is your true life's work? That is a question I think I cannot truly answer. So why do I not know my own mission? Am I lost, am I a sheep—or even a shepherd!—that has lost its little way? No, I think not. I am not lost because I am alive. Yes! I feel, I think, I see. How could I be lost when I am here at the pinprick of this moment? And besides, I am here looking at all of you looking at me looking at you. Now how lost could I be? Yes I did see today's front page picture and essay of me in *Time*, and *Newsweek*. And yes, it is true, like a common vagabond, I, Michelle Domingue found myself sleeping in parks and living on the streets amongst you here in this very city. I refused to use my father's credit card and just today tore it to bits, to pieces. It only took thirty seconds of continual folding!

"Now, now — please listen — I do not recommend that all should follow my example. It is a very hard and untrodden road to run.

"Here is my story then: I plunged headfirst into the belly of the whale, I lived in the shadow of tall buildings, I slept at the feet of old bums. I was with God at the window of St. Marks Pizza, I was the throne of some pigeons as I woke in the morning, I have sat on an uneasy bus bench, I suffered hunger for an hour before I stole a ripe plum. I saw the destruction of some bad guys on reruns of 'Branded,'

I strengthened myself in the land of orange groves, I stood with Mary Magdalene and refused a good prospect, I was in a lovely dress and I'm sure he couldn't resist. At first I was little and some called me Gigi, then for nine months I was in my mother's belly. At length I have become the genius citizen. Michelle the Divine, Oh Elias! I was the ass in the manger of the Lord. I am loquacious and given to speech impediment. I hung out in the sky over Rome and watched a galaxy of personalities fight from on high. I am a conundrum upon the face of the Earth and shall remain till some time way off in the future."

I took, finally, a deep and replenishing breath. So yes, then there were things that I did say to the multitudes at Carnegie Hall. Of course this little ol' rag of a speech was just something I tottled off the tip of my tongue. It was nothing, really. Just a last minute toss-off.

After the performance I sat alone in the dressing room facing myself in the mirror. There were bouquets of roses everywhere, nowhere in the room was there space to stand. That was why I, Michelle Domingue, sat now alone in my room in front of the mirror surrounded by lights. The crowd outside was still cheering, but I refused an encore. I had given so very much of myself, what more could I give?, unless I sold little pieces of skin that I naturally sloughed off, and that would be such a temporary curio.

There I sat and breathed and thought again of this week's appearance of my candid face upon the covers of *Time* and *Newsweek*. What could I think about it, really? It was done. Last week and now this week. Would it ever end? I thought fondly of those simpler days of me and Apricot and the Targa. Oh how things had changed. What a strange road my car was driving down and was it taking me home? Ken had somehow wiggled his way past the roses and rose bushes over to me at the mirror. What with all those smelly plants and the cramped room, we were pressed pretty tightly together, he sitting on my lap. Of course, this was perfectly natural.

"Ken, what am I to do with this cover story phenomenon that's happening to me, whatever am I to do?"

"Well, Michelle, of course I do know about these things, and here is my advice: I would like you to consider your image, I would like to construct a hard-boiled campaign that will take you into every home, hotel, dentist's office and country known to mankind. Now, of course, you know..."

"Oh, I know, go through the usual media *de rigeur*...me, Michelle Domingue and John Kennedy, Junior on *The National Enquirer*, me receiving the Nobel Peace Prize, Michelle Domingue a major suspect in a Hollywood murder case, me helping the few remaining victims of a catastrophic earthquake in Armenia, Michelle Domingue winning the big pot in the NewYork Lottery, making a really bad movie on a big budget that critics rave about, saving the survivors of a felled commercial airplane, dancing naked atop an Iraqi Mosque waving an American flag, caught on video in bed with the Pope...all that usual, common folderol. Ken really, isn't it enough to be, simply, a messiah to the people? Living proof of God's womanness alive and living on the Earth? Isn't it enough to heal tired, overanalyzed psyches as I have done?"

Ken stood up and stared at me agape.

"I have worked press and media so long now, Michelle Domingue, you would think I would know for certain. But quite frankly I do not know for sure that the world could enjoy and participate in your holy mission without the use of such spectacularities as those you've just mentioned. Honestly, I cannot imagine a Goddess-celebrity grabbing the eyes of the entire world at once, without the use of some of those common bread-and-circus tactics. I simply can't fathom it being done."

There was a scuffle at the door, it was opening and we could tell someone was attempting to enter. But with the wall-to-wall rose bushes, it would have been impossible to see who it was. Ken grabbed my hand and lead us through the rosy bramble, it scratching and clawing at our very fabric. He got us to the door.

There she was, Mary Rockett. Pop stars are always so different than you imagine them, so much more bumply real. She had pretty bad pimples. I'd guess she was about nineteen years old. Her hair was dyed pitch black. She wore tight checkerboard jeans and a dainty print top. No makeup, and a bright lime-green patent leather purse.

"Michelle Domingue, I've been wanting to meet you for so long now, I'm Mary Rockett. I hope I'm not interrupting or disturbing anything. I just wanted to meet you. Well I guess you're sorta one of my heroes." Mary then gave me an eight by ten glossy of herself, she signed it right there in front of us in a quick unreadable scrawl.

"Oh these are my bandmates Peggy, Ashley, and Fluffy. We just today released our new record and it's zooming up the hit parade. I got tired of playing with a bunch of guys, so I put this girl band together. We're called Meow."

The drummer Ashley was a frail girl, but I could intuitively detect she was a drummer and a hard-hittin' ferocious one at that.

"Yeah, Meow really rocks! Our hit single's called 'Pick Nose, Not Rose,' it's for a big movie out by the same title. Well, I'm a big fan of yours Michelle, I read everything I can about you. I've never asked for an autograph before, but could you sign my head with this indelible marker?"

"Why, I'd be happy to, Ashley, do you have to shave every day?"

"Oh, no way! I had electrolysis. I had it done everywhere, I hate hair!"

"Probably a good thing," I thought aloud. "No more pesky bikini shaving, underarm rashes..."

"Only thing I wanted to keep was my eyelashes and eyebrows. I consider eyebrows an art project."

I noticed now Ashley's eyebrows, yes she did have quite the artist's touch. An intriguing series of dots and dashes. Then it struck me.

"Why—does that say 'cheese is the mold of life' in Morse code?"

"All right! Yeah, it does, Michelle. That's my motto. Man, I love all your sayings. I've got Ken Jackowitz's book, the *Codex*. I look one up every single morning. You are so awesome! How do you think of that stuff?"

Then Fluffy chimed in.

"Yeah, and I've got the Apricot book. Did he screw you over or what...?"

"Ladies, ladies!" Ken thought that the mention of ol' Apricot would set my fireworks off.

"No, Ken, it's O.K. I feel all right about Ape, I just hope he gets the real recognition he deserves from the public, and that's for his Theories of Compensation. He's a genius, you know."

"Oh wow," (they all said) "no, we didn't know!"

Mary Rockett then gave me a big bundle of roses she'd brought me, and had me sign her arm.

"Michelle Domingue, here's a copy of Meow's version of 'Pick Nose, Not Rose.' I hope you like it. Really an honor to meet you."

And with that, Meow took their leave, and so did Ken and I. We grabbed a cab, leaving the room of roses for the janitorial staff, and made our way across Manhattan.

That night Ken, his wife Annie, and I stayed up for some time. Sitting around their fake polar bear table, sipping on Shirley Temples, chatting and sharing a good laugh. Ken was doing some famous people impersonations, and boy did he have me down to a t! Annie and I pretended to be interviewers, and he was fielding questions as Michelle Domingue. Of course, only a person such as Ken that knows the intricacies of my words and sayings could pull off such a stunt. Then Ken let me know that tomorrow morning I was to do myself at an interview. He said there could be as many as fifty press people there. Whew! He wanted me to be prepared for the media siege.

Ken and Annie then offered me an evening of sexual frolic with the both of them. Of course, I was most flattered, and gave it real thought before I answered. Certainly, they were very likable. Alas it was, in the end, God's decision. I was acting now for the history of all mankind, and thus my choices were not my own but those of the multitudes. No, there could be no joyful evening of sexual pleasures while the Earth's children needed my undivided attention and energy. I thanked them kindly. I certainly did not want my hosts to feel offended in any way, and offered that perhaps we could all sleep together in one bed and save the sexual explorations for another lifetime. (If indeed there is one. There were still so many questions I had for God.) They happily agreed to a chaste somnambulance. Within minutes we were fast asleep, pleasant smiles on our soporific faces.

I hadn't slept so well in days! I fell far and fast. I was drawn sleepily deeply into that faraway strangeland. And though I was resting genuinely, I was also traveling looking, and wondering. Even in my sleepful state I knew something of great importance was about to be unveiled to me. Yes, Yes. I was in a car, an old green 1967 Chevy station wagon, a guy from India decked out in jewels and royal wear was driving. He was driving over the speed limit and I was feeling like the car could go outta control. We were passing everyone on the road. "Don't worry, Michelle Domingue," the Hindu prince said. "It's under control, I've got the wheel and I'm used to going fast." Then I noticed that not only were we speeding, but we seemed to be the only ones moving! On closer inspection it was clear that things beside us were moving, only much slower. Slow mo. We were going so much faster than everything else that we were probably merely a breeze or a momentary blur of light that flashed in their eyes. What could be happening? "Where are we?" I finally uttered.

"Well, Michelle, we are on Earth still. We've stepped up our metabolisms and various biological/chemical functions to the speed of light. We needed to get somewhere fast."

"Well, what in the world? I just hope it's important. I need to get back to my sleep, I've an interview in eight hours."

"Oh, we won't be gone nearly that long. To you, mere minutes."

My Hindu companion was growing wider and older by the second. When he finally pulled the car over and put it in park he looked to be a good 300 pounds. All youth had vanished. Before me was a Buddha-looking fellow.

"Are you Buddha?" I inquired.

"I am one of a line of Buddha, yes."

"Oh, I thought so."

He was outta the car in a flash. A bird was suspended in the air overhead. Looked like a taxidermy statue levitating twenty feet above us. I looked away, and a minute later looked back to see its wings at a different angle. Oh, things were moving all right. I was reassured to know that I would be here only seconds.

"Come over here, Michelle."

"But it's dirty over there, that path is all muddy. Can't we stay here by the car?"

"No, Michelle, I'm afraid we can't. We must walk along this muddy path to get to the place that we are going."

"Place we are going? Where? But my lovely dress."

"No need to worry about your dress or the dirt, this is all unreal anyways. This is your dream. You'll wake up seconds from now clean and tidy. Follow me."

So I, Michelle Domingue, in the midst of my dream state, followed the self-professed Buddha along a sloppy clay path. Up and down a hill, chaparral land, a few trees, scrubby brush, high altitude sage. There, we approached the rocky face of a red and purple mesa. Looked like we were in the Southwest somewhere, maybe New Mexico. Buddha was looking over the stony strata on the upthrusting mesa ridge before us.

"Yes, this appears to be the spot."

"Just where we are standing?" I queried.

He touched the rock in front of him.

"Yes, yes,"

Then, before my very eyes, everything around me, the standstill birds, the unmoving breeze, the stick-stiff rattlesnakes, all of it began to shimmy and shake oh so slightly. Fading out of view then fluxing back into a funny kinda Georges Seurat-looking landscape, or perhaps Monet.

Anyway, one minute it was fuzzy and pointillist and then a blink of an eye later only TV static. What was Buddha up to and why was God condoning this? What could God be trying to convey to me with all this hocus pocus, that he couldn't just sit down and talk out? All theater tricks. God the barking ring leader and the saints a bunch of circus folk. Parting of the Red Sea, famine and pestilence, Satan's fiery furnace, all magic tricks! What's wrong with a good conversation? Well, here I was, Michelle Domingue, in the middle of a dream, watching the vision fade before me. Fade almost, then sway back into Impressionism. Then Buddha took my hand.

"Michelle, come in a little further."

I suppose I did. I didn't see anything at first. But I felt something all around me. Then my thoughts began to adjust, and I realized I was sharing the same space with Buddha and another presence. I heard in my head a lotta voices, including Buddha's.

"Michelle Domingue, this is my Teacher. He has honored us with his presence."

"Oh." I was a little surprised. "Where are we, then? Are we in heaven now?"

"No," the teacher's voice resounded in my head, "no, not heaven. I am a life form unknown to you organisms. I am at a much different metabolic rate. We may be like you in our atomic composition, but we have no bones, and have little need for respiratory systems. Our use of the same basic molecules such as proteins and nucleic acids, as you have, brought us a completely different existence. You know us as rock and think of us as an immovable object, and yet in our lives we move about as much as you organisms do. However, I do believe we live far longer than you. You respirating things come and go so quickly. Our carbon breaks down at a much slower rate. We are a seeming solid-state life. Though far away from us on this terrestrial globe, we know of far more solid life forms even than ourselves, those which live in and move about in electrical states, and others that float about in unending atmospheres."

Wow, I thought. There's just so much to know. Wow. Boy just think how awful it would be to fall in love with one of these mineral beings. Talk about unrequited, or could something work out? Well, only if it was really meant to be. Where there's a will, there's a way. I mean, here was Buddha having some kinda relationship with Rock. Like my ol' 5th grade teacher once said, if you imagine it, it can be. Actually he said, "anything you can imagine happening to a human being can, any disease, any mishap. The whole class shut up and thought on that. And who cared, this was all a three-second dream, and I would be back safely snug in bed with Ken and Annie in a fly's second.

Feeling Rock and Buddha all around me, I realized that we had indeed merged on a molecular level. I, Michelle Domingue, was a piece of mountain. It was truly a satisfying feeling.

"So," I wondered out loud, "what about the difference between a rock hill like you and a beach of sand? Do you organisms live in the soil?"

"No, Michelle, we are too broken down at that point. Our boundaries are far too difficult to explain. It is true this entire mesa constitutes my own body alone. But that is not so of all mountains and hills. There are those that live 'communally,' many entities as one."

I was thinking of the statue of David by Michelangelo. All that beautiful marble. "So," I posed, "A statue of marble could actually contain a spirit or, uh, organism of your kind, and perhaps even more than one of you?"

"If the life-giving materials are there, it may be so. Though we need far less water than you, for you beings are practically small oceans, we still work with a solvent system. And water is very important to our existence."

I wondered if the Rock beings in David knew they were in the shape of a human being. Did one of them know they were the shape of a man's genitalia? Seemed to me after what Rock was just saying it could be quite possible that David was not a living entity—due to lack of water. Perhaps a better example of living statue could be Mt. Rushmore. Rocks still attached to their mountain. And could these mineral beings ever get to the point where they could move themselves quick enough to speak through the Washington or Lincoln face? That would be a great unifying day for the world. A new kingdom of families, genuses and species to explore and record. Science. I thought of Apricot. A senseless gray matter knee jerk. I jolted back into the sleeping non-reality world of Rock and Buddhas. I was finding it slightly difficult to breathe, and knew that my two-minute dream was near done. I knew too that there was something of significance which Rock had to convey to me.

"Michelle Domingue, yes, I do have something to tell, you are quite correct."

Obviously, Rock could read all my thoughts. It was as though every thing I thought and felt was not my own. All a movie.

"It is true, Michelle, I know your thoughts, and I am quite sure that the mineral spirits in the statue of David are concerned with loftier subjects than their exterior shape. However, I would like to impart to you this one thought, Michelle Domingue. Now think. The world of people and beings and media has been very good to you. All has worked as one to create that which you are. This is God's plan. There was a calling and your foot fit the shoe. Here in the rock world we have a famous saying which is basically translated as, "Gravity got 'em." Gravity can be a very destructive force to a rock. It's one thing for a rock spirit to break apart from its community and quite another for it to crumble into pieces of sediment. As I've already told you, we exist as any number of shapes and sizes but our life on Earth ends once we've broken down into simple soil.

So gravity can be destructive, a force that can disrupt a mortal life! Now, of course, it is also gravity that keeps us together and pins us to this world so that we are not just bits of minute asteroid floating solo in the heavens. So gravity as a force has its good and its bad. That is its job. There is much gravity in your situation, Michelle Domingue."

With that, the voice ended. Buddha touched my arm, and I felt myself tumbling, it seemed, end over end from dark toward the light. Nothing other than the light was visible. I suppose the two-minute dream was up, cuz I was now comfortably back in bed with my host and hostess, the three of us together in a pleasant sleeping embrace. The lesson over, I could now fall into a deeper, more replenishing, autumnal slumber.

Chapter Seven

Rest, rest my pretties...

For breakfast Annie had a number of items displayed on the kitchen table. Breakfast Bars, Hostess Twinkies and Ding Dongs. Chocolate Gems Donuts, Hostess Apple and Berry Pies. To drink, our choice of Tang, Ovaltine, and Nestle's Strawberry Quik. There were some dietary foodstuffs as well.

It all looked so delicious, I couldn't make up my mind what to eat, so I had a little bit of everything.

"Really, Annie, you shouldn't have gone to all the trouble on my account, this is far more than I can eat."

"Oh really, it's nothing, Michelle. Ken and I can finish up what you don't eat, just help yourself. We have pretty healthy appetites around here. So believe me, no guilt will be needed for the starving kids in China. We make sure to eat every crumb, isn't that so honey?"

"Oh yeah, Michelle, she's right, we do enjoy our breakfasts around here. A good breakfast should zip you right out the door, and after a meal of Ding Dongs, berry pies, and strawberry milk, boy, I just want to go! It gives me the lift I need each morning. Annie's so smart, and there's no muss or fuss in the kitchen."

"Oh no," chimed in Annie. "Oh, I don't believe in that old 'women's work' idea. I just wanna take the plastic wrap off, eat, and go! Ken and I are pretty much two of a kind in that way. I think maybe we're a real model for living in today's world. Everything moves so fast. You just gotta keep up, and a good breakfast helps us do that."

So Ken, Annie and I sat at their dining room table on the ninth floor overlooking New York with the early day sun streaming in, eating all those good American delicacies. Ate up every last crumb. The morning paper was passed around, and besides my face on the front of the *Times*, we found an article inside on Mary Rockett and Meow. Seems their second single just hit the number 1 slot, knocking their previous song outta that position. The new hit being the catchy "Rest, Rest, my Pelvis."

Annie was real excited about that.

"Wow! I just heard that song yesterday on WFMU. I didn't know who it was, but what a song. I called the station right away, and sure enough they said it was Mary Rockett's new band, Meow. What a great song, it makes me feel so... happy!

'Rest, rest my pelvis! La, la, la-la-la.

Rest, rest my pretty! La, la, la!' Empowering!"

"Oh Annie, I think that song was on the clock radio when we woke up. I kept hearing "rest my pretties," and thinking about the wicked witch and the field of poppies.

"Well Michelle, the article says: 'the song conjures up strong Oz imagery juxtaposing poppies with modern heroin addiction. Witches and junkies.' And here Mary's words are being compared to Shakespeare's sonnets. What! Oh wow, this is kinda strange..."

"What?" I wondered out loud.

Annie gave Ken a conspicuously strong look. A kind of oh-shit-help-me-out look. What was going on?

"What?" I repeated. Something strange was being conjured within me. Something powerful. My esophagus began vibrating, literally buzzing. Calmly I got up, walked to the open window on the ninth floor, bent my head out into the New York autumn coolness and released all anticipations, clogged unspeakables, jammed feelings, Ding Dongs, Twinkies and Strawberry milk. Released, cleared, I could breathe easy again. I closed the window and walked back to the breakfast table. Still something wasn't right. Ken was mumbling, stumbling over a simple word or two.

"Ah, well, if...well, Michelle. The article here says Mr. Apricot was seen hanging out with Mary and Meow at the afterhours club Robots. The writer speculates that Mary and Mr. Apri—"

"Well," I blurted, "perhaps, but of course he is married now and living on Long Island. So that's between him and his wife. I, Michelle Domingue, am merely an acquaintance. I await God's word on spousal designation."

Spousal designation, indeed. And when was God going to come forward with this vital piece of information? And was today the day I would meet Jesus and find out just what that word Christ means? I mean Jesus, or rather Joshua (pronounced Yashua), was this guy's real name, what's the Christ word for? Is it sort of like "swami"or...how can a people have used the word Christ for so long now and not know exactly what it means?! I fingered a passed-over bite of Twinkie and popped it into my mouth.

"Ken, let's go, I've got a stop to make before we go to the press conference."

We threw on our raincoats and grabbed umbrellas. Out the ninth floor window we could see thunderheads gathering and the paper had predicted rain.

Oh that day, oh that blustery day. The clouds were rolling in from the west. They'd accumulated from somewhere, from thatta way, the hump of land called America. These were good ol' U.S. clouds, nothing Atlantean about them. And they were coming on strong. I could tell it was a powerful ion day. If indeed it was to rain, it was to be no ordinary deluge. More a dispersion of energies piggy-backing on the H_2O element. Soon they would come, soon. But now, only the fist of clouds, the heavy breathing sky. Ken and I spotted and ran for a cab.

"Fourteenth Street please, and hurry."

"Yes, ma'am, where do you go especially, on Fourteen?"

"The old church between First and A!"

Ken, straightening his overcoat, looked at me questioningly.

"But Michelle, there's little time, our appointment, our press meeting, the top media dogs..."

"Ken, first things first."

"Say, Miss," it was the cabby, he wanted my attention. "Say, your face, you are famous Messiah. Ah yes! Oh my your face and words are so good and I wanted to see you last night at Carnegie. But hey, you know this was work time. You are something very special. Only you, Michelle Domingue, the prophet Jesus, the holy Mohammed (and Um Kulthum) are so dear to me. I should pull over the car now, wipe your feet, and offer you blessings."

It was a lovely sentiment, and certainly my patent leathers could've used a good shine. But I had to say "thank you, no." There was too much dignity shining from that nut brown face that reflected at me from the taxi's rear-view mirror. The spirit of Egypt was pouring through him. While sitting there at the signal, the cabby and I looked thoughtfully, deeply into the rear-view mirror and into one another's soul windows. Brown eyes met blue. In an instant I was transported to a time far far off in the remote past. I felt myself floating, yes, floating on a reed boat down the Nile. And there I was, me, this woman, not Michelle Domingue, but this other woman weeping — my hands to my face. My dead lover's body beside me and then magically his lifeless body is resurrected and becomes a canary — yellow — and flutters away. Pyramids loom in the sandy expanse. The heavy weight of future time rests upon my shoulders. The gravity of the first brick. Ah, gravity, the dream last night! The dream? Or was it simply a sleeping reality?

Oh yes, the gravity of the situation. The world's woes troubles hopes and fears resting upon my very shoulders. Trouble being that I had very slim shoulders. I had thought once while a teenager that I would perhaps look into becoming a supermodel. Dad went so far as to take me into a Barbiecon Modeling Agency where I was promptly prodded, measured, questioned, then brought into a small and heavily perfumed room while a Madame sat behind a round metal table and tapped her perfect red fingernails gently upon its metalness. The middle-aged Madame bent over my test results. "Michelle Domingue, you are narrow, perhaps not of mind. Just simply narrow. From your shoulders on down darling you are narrow. Your weight is this and you're that tall and we will need some thousand dollars from your very nice father." We told Madame we would think it over, and ultimately decided no. There was quite honestly little room for "narrowness" in the pages of popular pose. I reconciled myself to a more prestigious commission in life. I hoped one day to be a wife. Had that hope passed me by? Was I wagering a fruitless gamble, wasted on unheard words from God, from Jesus or...Here! in this Yellow Cab, a symbol of divinity, an ancestor of the holy prophet Mohammed...did he have a message for me, Michelle Domingue?

"Miss, here is your Catholic church. This is Fourteenth. OK? You OK? You musta fainted or somethin'. Yes, we're here."

We were here. Mohammed had brought me to the mountain. Ken paid our driver and I thanked him for his gift of true inspiration by handing him a Ding Dong I had socked away from breakfast. He nodded to me graciously. We were so pleased with one another. The cabby opened the door for me, took my lily pale hand and helped me out. For one last minute we exchanged a deep yellow vibrational level of eye contact and I left him with this sputtering of words:

BROWN BEAN IN A BLUE BEAN JAR. BRUISED BANANAS IN AN APPLE BOWL. PRICE TAG HANGING ON A PLASTIC FLOWER.

But now I was off, here was the church! I marched in boldly, feeling like Joan of Arc. A mission!

Ken straggled somewhere limply behind me. There were a few locals lighting candles at the saints or praying at particular Jesus stations. None of that in-between stuff for me, I was going straight to the top —the Boss—up to the front altar. There were the flowers, the golden vases, a table with a white cloth and a bottle of red wine and a golden cup. I knew, I just knew this was God's little way of welcoming me. Much the same as our cookie offerings to Santa at Xmas. I was Santa and visiting the home of God. Of course God is well off and has many homes, this just being one of an assortment, and yet through something in the ethers I was aware God was at *this* moment at *this* house.

The wine wasn't bad at all. Perhaps a bit sweet. It was from a California vineyard, a symbolic nod to my roots. God had left some cookies too, though they were bland, quite tasteless. Yes, of course, I was just like Santa. Perhaps my gift to God's house was simply my presence or a thing which would spring forth from me but was yet unknown. The sounds of New York began to fade away. Ken had found himself a saint to sit near and was busy discussing something to its stoical stone face in a far-off voice, sounding like politics. I filled the gold cup again with more sweet vino and gulped the stuff down, ate more cookies and drank again. How good of God. Then, moving towards me, came a slightly blurred vision in white. Oh. I thought, it must be God! Or is it merely Gabriel summoning me to the Lord's private chamber? I stood at Heaven's door and awaited word. The figure in white looked me over, not unhappily but still not smiling. An ambivalent God? Was this the man I was to marry? It was so hard to see his face, for the candles before me on the white-clothed table were dancing about wildly, obscuring my vision, putting a fuzzy glare on all things of a material nature. It seemed as though night had fallen suddenly, yet I knew it to be a bright harvest day morn outside this holy structure. Strangely all light seemed sucked in by these very "candles," as though they had an exceptionally dense gravity and within them contained the pinpoint of singularity. (Ah, again gravity! How prophetic of the Rock.) The white vision of a man was closer now, having been drawn into the circular orbit of light. If this was God, then God was now manifest as a stern pock-marked face floating vividly above a white mantle. "God" spoketh:

"Woman what do you intend before the Altar of Him?"

It must be an angel. Someone speaking for his Allness.

"Well, your Holiness, I am but a mere mortal that has been summoned here by...well—" I gulped. "...your Boss. For some, God knows what, reason."

"Put down that holy vessel immediately and follow me."

We went into some back room area that was flickering with the light of a dozen candles. And sat at an old wooden desk. He prepared to speak.

"You seem so familiar to me."

"God probably told you I was coming. My name is Michelle Domingue. You may have seen me in the papers or magazines."

"Oh yes. Yes, you Michelle Domingue are the Great Prophetess/Healer of our time. Oh yes, you were so out of context, it took me a minute." His old face smiled, warmed right up.

"Well, Michelle Domingue, what can a mere humble servant of our Lord do for you?"

"I've come to speak with God hisself."

"Well, yes, everybody does come here for that. Perhaps one of the holy stations or..."

"Oh no, I'm ready to go direct. One on one. Interface with the Big Guy. I'm ready for you to introduce me."

Really this angel in white, aging though he was, perhaps even 80 years old, was quite likable. Yes, I'd taken a real hankering to him. Certainly, God was being well served by this Great Doorkeeper, this Divine Butler. This old stony countenance that watched all things come and go like a ruined obelisk left to stand in the long desert of existence. He turned from me abashed by my keen eye.

"Oh," he heaved, "even if I could... Michelle, I have done wrongs in my time. My thoughts have touched innocents and I have wronged humanity from a high and trusted position. I am hardly worthy of mortality, mostly I hide here in this room asking forgiveness for wrongs, sins of my wild and impetuous youth. Boy could I drink! I could outdrink any heathen Methodist, Baptist or Catholic in nothin' flat. Ah, those were the bad old days. But then when I drank I thought such heretical visions, demonic! And when pretty young things came into the confessional, oh, back then, I could hardly think straight. Michelle, I don't know how those other priests do it, pushing down those unclean thoughts. In my mind, I touched almost everybody. My naked thoughts, unclean desires, groped at girls and boys alike. I got so scared after some time that I didn't know if I'd touched them in reality or not. I simply couldn't tell the difference. To this day I just don't know. Therefore I keep myself alone here in this work chamber or my very small sleeping quarters. I haven't heard a confession in years, I haven't spoken to a soul in at least ten, Michelle, and yet now here I am blabbing away to you. I felt your presence before I saw you. Something drew me out into the church this morning. Oh, Michelle Domingue, and it was you!"

The dear angel put his head in my lap and cried an ancient deluge of deeply dredged waters. Tears held for so long they had become as briny as the waters of the Dead Sea. A good ten minutes rolled by, the emotional storm didn't abate. Finally I pulled his head from my lap and brought it up to eye level.

A FITTER IS A PERSON THAT FITS A THING THAT IS SUITABLE.

It sputtered out of my mouth involuntarily. It was almost embarrassing. A touching, emotional and private moment, and then from my lips a great monolith of a phrase such as that. I nearly blushed. The good words seemed to be gobbled and digested by my elderly priest friend, for his sobbing stopped suddenly.

"Michelle Domingue, you are truly a great one. These words that emanate from you are deeply powerful constructs. Far more than mere human words. It's as though they resonate with *The* Word. The vowels and consonants *feel* so wholly familiar. It is as though God Himself has spoken! The primordial sound struck, BONG!, at the beginning of time, vibrates on and on. Lives! Still lives and yet how often does it pass this Earthly way, how long for the original sound to make its way around the circumference of the universe and at last come back to us? A passing comet. Each pass growing a mere bit fainter, a longer stretch of time, more difficult for our complex evolution to understand."

There was something to what he was saying. Yet I, Michelle Domingue, had no time to unravel its undeniable mystery. I had a press conference to attend, and Ken Jackowitz was waiting for me in the whale ribs of the church. No doubt he had finished his political debate with the cemented form of some saint. And here was this priest before me, ex-priest, invisible churchman, sinner holy man, hermit, regular guy living an unregular life. I couldn't just leave him there. Somehow I felt compelled to bring him on my trek across town with Ken and myself. Perhaps he had more golden words to spin and could fit another important moment into the book of my life. If he was willing, I certainly would let him give it a try.

Ken had long finished his sainted dissertation and was at the big door of the sanctuary, dipping a hanky in the holy water, dabbing his sweat-riddled forehead.

"Geez, Michelle, I, I thought you'd never alight. The time is getting..."

"Oh, Ken, don't talk to me of time. Not when there are nebulae and star clusters where whole suns are being born — another falling into a state of collapse to perhaps become a siphon of light. Proteins and acids coagulating just so on a desolate planetscape pockmarked by astral dirt clods and yet in a moment the right combination could bring about a true, new atmosphere!"

"But Michelle...!"

"Ken," I took a deep breath and surveyed the situation. "Here is a hermit of the church, he will accompany us to our next destination."

Michelle," Ken queried in a worried way, "wherever could that be?"

Chapter Eight

Not even I, Michelle Domingue, was certain where we were to go. Yet I wasn't ready for my media siege and I had a funny kinda feeling that ol' Priesty here had something up his sleeve. First off, I wasn't yet convinced that he wasn't God. How clever it would be for the Holy Spirit to mask himself as a feeble ol' hermit hidden away in a low-profile cathedral. And even if he wasn't God, he was still a likable old guy that maybe could point me in God's direction. The taxi came and we moved uptown.

"Pull over here, cabbie, can you change a fifty?" Our priestly pal tossed a bill over the faded green upholstery.

"Yeah," the driver wiggled his Irish wool cap, licked his pointer finger and started counting out ones and fives. We were somewhere in the Chelsea district, in the 20s, idling in front of a closed movie theater. Newspapers blew down the sidewalk, tumbleweed style. Next to the broken-down cinema a woman was leaning out an apartment window looking at us.

"Say listen, I gotta go in for a few minutes." My new-found holy friend fumbled with his robe and chucked his change away somewhere in its folds. "Why don't you two wait across the street there at the Salty Lion while I take care of a little business? Shouldn't be but a few minutes. Tell Joe you're friends of mine, and they'll provide you with a beverage."

No one was inside the Salty Lion. Not even Joe. It was a black hole of a bar with no windows and an occasional wall lamp from the '50s providing a shadowy twilight. A radio station pleasantly hummed a crackly version of "Moonlight Serenade" from a dusty gray mono speaker.

"Isn't this place lovely?" I thought aloud. "I mean, it's just like a movie."

"Frankly, Michelle, I think this place could use some airing out. It stinks of ancient vomit and dead cigarettes."

"Yes it does, I just find it refreshing, so real, just beautiful, ah breathe that air."

"I think you could provide a service, Michelle Domingue, by healing this foul cave of its dark unidentifiable grief."

"Ken Jackowitz, you must know by now that whatever healing process is done by me or perhaps anyone is not out of choice but done by spontaneity of spirit. If this dive bar is ready for healing, it shall be, no sooner. Besides, I find this dark, dank smelly old place charming in some way."

What I was thinking was ol' Priesty had suggested we visit the Salty Lion because it was a simple, inconspicuous place to meet the Greatest One. A very large woman walked out from behind a beaded curtain. Her makeup had been applied with a precise hand. She was shuffling cards from one hand to the other.

"Oh my, I'm so sorry. I didn't know anyone was out here. I was in the little girls' room. I had a little tinkle to take." She giggled. "Oh my, oh I'm getting such strong waves from you two, oh God the magnetic fields are going haywire around here. I've never seen anything like it. God, can I get you a drink?"

Twice the word God. Was it a sign? We ordered two Pepsis. And told her we were friends of a hermit priest from Fourteenth Street.

"Oh I shoulda guessed. My name's Joe. Josephine. But honey, there's some kinda energy comin' offa you that could light Staten Island. Here, let me do your cards."

The extremely large woman wiped her lands on her flower print dress and reshuffled the dirty well-worn cards. How was I to know that she would lay out the skeletal framework that defined what I was and was still to become. Sometimes even the darkness shows us to the light.

The radio announcer had one of those old voices that you can only hear from male broadcasters over the age of 60, a nostalgic, self-assured and bland quality. Joe stopped shuffling and stared out into the half light with a listening expression. The announcer rambled on and then, "that's right folks the Pope will be visiting us here in Gotham. Specifically to see the UN about those numerous UFO sightings world-wide. But if it's a divine glimpse you want, well get yourself over to the East River by noon. Let's show em that good ol' American spirit. That's right today only, folks." His voice trailed off and the Lennon Sisters's voices boomed in with a perky version of "Over There." Joe cut the cards and had me cut them the third time she took a long chug off her beer and started picking cards and laying them in a kind of wheel pattern. All became quiet except for Ken's crunching from a bowl of store-bought green popcorn. Then that ceased. We all looked at the cards, all eyes cast downward awaiting their wisdom. The Great Big woman seemed to loom over us even larger. Seemed like we shrank down to the size of children in our highchair bar stools and she grew to be the giant she really was. Her eyes were like saucers, flying saucers. There was so much activity in those eyes that they appeared to be hovering like buzzing bees in front of her face. Her nose pro-truded out like a massive hanging boulder, we waited for the avalanche. Her words came from a dark cave of mouth as if issuing from some subterranean crea-ture that lived in the hull of the body form, a crea-ture never exposed to the daylight or starlight of this world. A mole being that lived and moved within this human host named Joe.

My father used to say as I'd sit with him in his study, he puffing away on his pipe, "Michelle, this is one strange ol' world we live in, things seem to be one thing, and turn out to be another. Take the people that move through our lives. You and me, we know ourselves to be real. Mom, Gramma and Grandad Domingue — we know they're real 'cause we've hugged, touched and seen them in all sorts of situations. But the nondescript people, the everyday folk that we don't know that pass by us at the mall or the grocery store, how can we know they are real? We can't say for certain that they are like us Perhaps they are just a side of cardboard, all painted to look like a person and we never see their brown paper side—only the colored front. Yes, perhaps there are lots of cardboard people out there, and just a few of us here carrying on human lives."

Josephine of the Salty Lion was not what she appeared to be. Joe was a small dark animal of a person that shrank far within the depths of the large cardboard cut-out Joe.

Oh dear," the huge woman exclaimed. "A man is to re-enter your life, Michelle, and the cards show a very strong disruption. Not a father figure. But a very aggressive man of your past. Oh dear, very soon."

Aggressive? Could it be Apricot, my sweet Mr. Apricot aggressive? I knew from the depths of my heart chakra that Mr. Apricot and I were to tangle again in some respect, though aggressively, no, I thought not. However I almost had no time to finish this very thought when a middle-aged hunched-at-the-shoulder man loomed in the open doorway of the Salty Lion and blocked our light. The old drinkery became a darker shade of black. Joe took in a deep startled breath and collected her cards. She had shrunk down to her true human-size and Ken and I had blown back up to our actual size, sitting normally now on our bar stools. The man stood there in the doorway swaying from side to side, creating moving streams of incoming light and bold blocks of shadow. He finally decided to join us and saddled up the bar. The radio was quiet for a moment, then the music to *The Good, the Bad and the Ugly* came over the airwaves.

"Say there, ol' gal, I'll take a shot o' whiskey and a Rolling Rock." He grumbled his words out. We couldn't see him too well in the dark.

"Name's Bob, ol' gal."

Josephine was shuffling around trying to find a clean whiskey glass. She looked pretty nervous. Maybe she knew this guy. "Name's Bob, and I been lookin' high and low, don't know where all I had to go to find you."

He took his hat off, revealing a perfectly bald and slightly familiar head, then turned and stared directly at me, Michelle Domingue. Ken was

138

between us and was so nervous he knocked the green popcorn to the ground and fumbled his Cola glass, spilling its icy contents on the wooden counter.

This man of the shadows laughed one wicked laugh and I actually felt bad for my friend Ken.

"Listen," I interrupted, "we don't need your bad vibes here. Why don't you just drink your drink and scram."

"Hah! Leave, you say, but I don't think so girly don't you remember me, Hon? Take a good look. I bought you that goddamn dress you're wearing now!"

"So what, you spent 35 dollars at a sale. Yeah, I remember you alright. What's up, you got a hair up your butt?"

"I looked all over this damn city. Followed you everywhere. Even paid good money, five bucks to see you at Carnagie. And did they let me back stage? No! Who do you think you are. I bought you that dress. Haven't you got my letters, all my letters?"

"Oh wow," Ken shrank further away from the bald man. "Michelle, he's been writing you via the AAMD for days now. This guy's a nut," he whispered.

A nut eh? Yes, indeed I did remember this character. Only two days ago, in the midst of my mid-book crisis, I'd met him and allowed him to buy me a Coke, a slice and even this dress. This dress I'd come to know and love. I'd made it mine. Its molecular structure had commingled with my own. And there could even be a palimony agreement at work here.

But this guy with the bald head and the hairy elbows. It appeared he wanted something more from me than dress repossession. His eyes pulsed and bobbed in and out of their sockets as he stared at me. Yes, this odd specimen of a man wanted the pure white soul of Michelle Domingue.

"Whatever you are Girly, I still don't know. Some kinda homo or lesbian or sumpthin…"

There was a large cat tattoo on his left arm between the elbow and the hand—you could barely see it through the forest of dark hair. His bicep was undulating with his every word, restless, like a runner in the stops before the gun blows.

"But I don't care if you're girl or boy. Your fella here better just step aside now and let Papa take you to the car. Come on with me. I don't want to have to throw you over my shoulder, Babe."

The stunning thing about this little scenario was that muscle-arm didn't even realize he was talking to me, Michelle Domingue Present Day Messiah. Jesus probably didn't have to put up with this bullshit. Still I was interested to see how this form of humanity expressed itself. He pushed Ken out of his chair and grabbed me about the shoulders. Josephone lurched in the murk, horrified.

"Why, I'll teach you a thing! You ain't gonna set up no man again. Posing as a street waif prostitute. You got my hopes up and I couldn't get 'em down. Then you left me hanging with no sex or nothin'!

Why I oughta..." He pulled me off the chair and took a swing at my head. Thinking quick, I ducked and clapped my hands.

He took another swing and I did the same thing. "There Girly, that oughta teach you to mess with a man." Then I grabbed a catsup bottle and splashed some tomato red on my cheek. He looked satisfied, as though he'd accomplished something. Of course, I learned this kind of quick stage-fight maneuver in my one year of acting at Junior College. I believe it to be an ancient form of martial art, one that makes the aggressor believe he has done an act of violence, but in reality has not. Ken looked on, shocked. I took a deep breath, now our fun was over and it was time for me to heal the wounded.

AIN'T NOTHIN' BUT THE RUMBLE AND ROAR OF THE TWO- AND FOUR-DOOR.

I pulled a hanky from my patent leather purse and dabbed the catsup off my cheek. The bald man had fallen in a heap upon the ground. He was not a sympathetic character and had a lot of making up to do, generally he was not a very likable guy from the get go. But I do remember when I first met him on St. Marks, and that mutt ran up and befriended him. That had indicated that there must be some kind of good hidden far below the surface.

Yet, I found it quite difficult to dredge up the pure compassion that I'd become accustomed to in myself. A rage was building in me, even though the bald perpetrator was prostrate before me, falling into the abyss of his own misdoings. I felt like Jesus the day he turned tables over at the temple. Except that I wanted to turn this table and kick it in the shin. I couldn't believe the anger that was surging through my veins. A tiger was running amok behind my eyes. It was dizzying. I grabbed at a chair, wanting to pick it up and smash it over the prostrate sinner. Instead, I steadied myself and took in a breath. Was I falling from grace? How could I be angry?! Me, Michelle Domingue, Modern Day Messiah. I was struggling on that well-worn path trodden by Jesus, but God still hadn't introduced us. Geeze, I could use a mentor now. My poor head was spinning and I collapsed into the wooden chair. The anger was a pulse hammering its nail into the tree of my being. How could I be so angry? What had happened? Where had I failed? Did I bring this on myself? How could I be a beacon of purity now? How could I administer to others, when the same evil root of despair lay within me too? Woe is me, all was so dark and ill-defined. Was all lost? And then in that dark hole of hopelessness, pit of no return, shone down a face so pure and white and well-lit that I could've sworn I was not at all in the den of the Salty Lion, but perhaps at the end of the long corridor of Heaven. The face shone with a luminescence that is altogether impossible to describe. A halo of a face, and then it spoke to me.

"Michelle Domingue, do not attempt to speak. I have only a few words to offer you and I hope they will be some comfort. Go forth unto your people and administer unto them. Your pain is theirs, their joy is yours. Life is short enough, get a boyfriend, enjoy your life. Get married if you want. Whatever, do your job and enjoy your life. Ah, this anger thing, don't dwell on it, big deal, go on now, say your words to your people, administer to them, have a good time. And that Apricot boy, he wasn't so bad, huh? Think it over, you could do worse. Jesus and you are not a good match. The love signs, the asteroids, are all wrong. Go on now..."

The words fell over me like manna, like muons, their tiny particles bombarding me from the depths of the cosmic circumference. I began to come to, to cognate on the idea that I was back at the Salty Lion and someone was leaning over me with a withered old hand and a glass of water. Was I, could I still be peering into the face of the Angelic Host? I blinked back into the now of the moment and saw the face to be my own dear priestly Hermit. Somehow his own countenance and that of the divine being had seemed to blur just for an instant, as though they'd been one and the same.

"Michelle, Michelle dear you will feel so much better if you take a sip of the waters."

My spirit was landing softly onto the runway of my material body, and I felt the gentle contact. Yes,

I would take a drink. The water went down hot and burned the wall of my esophagus, plunked with a splash into my stomach and gave me a mighty feeling of vitality. I looked up again at the befrocked old man, looming whitely over me. He offered a thoughtful smile.

"Strong water," I sputtered. He nodded.

I got right to the heart of the matter.

"Say, I've been wondering something and now, well, I just had a mighty vision and your face looks..."

"Oh Michelle, you're still faint, take another sip and we will be off again. The masses..."

"And the media," Ken chimed in...

"are waiting for you."

I took another deep sip of the raging water. "Yes they are waiting, aren't they? Well, let us be off then..."

"But," Josephine interrupted, "what about this heap of a man before you Michelle that has done you wrong and is now shining your shoes?" Indeed he was shining my shoes, giving them a special buff with his salty tears and doing a very good job. Strangely, I no longer felt torn and tattered with feelings of anger. All was forgiven.

"Indeed," I thought aloud, "what is to be done with him?" I pulled a dollar bill from my purse and meekly laid it on the ground at his eye level. He thanked me profusely, the shiny dome of his head dipping in obeisance. The radio was crackling out another fine old tune, a rousing interpretation of "76 Trombones," and I took it as a cue.

"Let us be off." I plunged my pointer finger toward the lit doorway. We shouted our goodbyes to the very large Joe and her Salty Lion, then Ken, the Hermit and myself were once again weaving crosstown in a California sun-yellow cab.

Chapter Nine

It was a leaf-falling, cool clear noon as we approached the throngs. We could see their monstrous numbers filling entire boulevards ahead of us. Ken had us pull the cab over and dashed to a pay phone. On his return there came with him a very concerned face.

"Michelle, our media siege has been altered. I'm not sure what to think of this, but, but..."

Ken was afraid to spit it out. I grabbed him good and solid by the shoulders and shook him. Even if Ken couldn't get the words up himself, choking as he was, I could Heimlich them out of him. I swatted him on the back a few times, then got him into a headstand on the sidewalk next to the cab. Finally the words fell from his knotted stomach.

"The Pope's people have been looking for you all morning," he coughed. "The Pope, yes, the Pope wants an audience with you, Michelle Domingue."

Whatever that could mean, I did not know. What could the great Catholic Pooh-Bah want from a simple folksy messiah such as myself? I only knew that it could possibly provide an intriguing turn in the memoirs of the life of me, Michelle Domingue.

What is it about autumn? Oh, I adore it so. Leaves and leaflets leave their trees and dance at the insistence of the persistent breeze. Skittle scuttle down the street kicked around by the city feets. And the woe-is-me moaning of the wind, winding its way from Earthly end to end.

Dear dearest mother of whom I barely remember, died in my wee-est of years in the dearest of days. Autumn is embossed on my emotive brain, a postmarked stamp stuck to the envelope of my life. Halloween swept its witch-broom in and whisked her away. Instead of a mother, I was left with a paper bag of cardboard-cut-out witches, ghosts, humorous-looking ghouls, festive trinkets to toy with and hang in the window. But the Halloween baubles simply could not take my mother's place, and though I asked for a refund, the deal had been sealed, the toys were mine to keep. My mother was gone. In the cool of the evening, by the heat of the day, in the dim of the in-between, I alone must make my wee and little way.

She, mother of me, Michelle Domingue, had once been a world-famous archaeologist, discovered and uncovered many fabulous sights from the Easter Island "Birdman" to baked bread in the ovens of Pompeii to the remains of Ur and Nineveh and other

Sumerian sites. When I was but a youngster, Mother was often out at local Southern California desert digs unearthing age-old Indian dwellings. In her last week of life, she had found a provocative burial ground dating back to the earliest known Los Angeles findings when, alas, she was struck with the curse. She had somehow contracted the dreaded Valley Fever. One day she lay at home on our brown floral-patterned couch, a funny look on her face. The next day she was gone and then the bag of Halloween knickknacks mysteriously appeared. Damn, if only...I hadn't wished for them.

We'd seen them back at the cab while Priesty and I were trying to knock those Popish words from Ken's tummy stronghold. We saw them moving black-suitedly through the crowd of colors, obviously looking for me, Michelle Domingue. I needed a few moments of silence to ready myself for my Pope visitation. The kind of silence a used bookstore could provide me.

"Are you Michelle Venus Domingue of Los Angeles?"

They'd found us. Twelve men with nice suits on, ties and new haircuts.

"Why yes, I am Michelle V. Domingue of the original Domingue lineage. And this is Ken Jackowitz and my dear Priesty friend."

They'd found us hiding behind a very tall row of used books, the scrambled poetry section of a small and dim bookstore. I pulled down a complete Shelley and fluttered through till I found my favorite passage, then I looked those men deeply in each and every eyeball and recited:

"My name is Ozymandias, King of Kings:

Look on my works, ye Mighty, and despair!"

The Suited Group were obviously not well receiving of these poetical words, for they rushed to my side, grabbed the book, dashed it upon the ground and proceeded to clasp my hands behind my back with some metallic restraining device.

Poor Ken fainted on the spot. Fortunately, Priesty caught his fall and saved him from head injury.

"Who in the world do you think you are, frightening a little poetry-perusing trio such as ourselves? You should be ashamed of yourselves." The priest really gave it to 'em. Gave them the whole authority-of-God vibe and everything. Yes, we were standing there in the thick of the Poetry section. Not only due to my particular circumstances, but because of where we were, I could feel the deprivation and persecution swarming about me. It had been there on the shelves dormant for who knows how long, waiting for a breeze to set it aflight. A ghost awaiting a living host.

Just to the right of Poetry by chance were the History shelves, with a specialization in Middle Ages. Quite suddenly, and for no apparent reason, an old volume fell at our feet in a dusty puff. A suit kicked at it till it turned over front side up.

The mysterious tome was so old and loosely bound, it was a miracle that it survived the fall. Priesty went to its side and picked it up tenderly.

"Oh my gracious!" he exclaimed, "Oh, my!"

"Well, what is it, my friend?" We all wanted to know, it was in some confounded foreign language.

"My dear," the priest sputtered out amidst a tear of joy, "it is none other than the *Cartulaire General de L'Ordre du Temple*, written in the year of our Lord 1913. A first edition! What a find."

One of the stern-faced suits snatched the odd volume from the pure white hands of my dear priest friend.

"This is a sign from on high," he chirped to his comrades. "Only a heretical old book like this would uncover itself while we are amongst the unclean, this... this deviltress and these demonic disciples."

Ken was just beginning to come to, sitting up and swatting the book dust from his clothes.

"Demonic? Devils? But this means nothing to me. I'm Jewish."

"You best watch your P's and Q's, wicked one. As for the book, it will sit in a prestigious position amongst the countless other Heretical Antichrist volumes, lost to the world in the labyrinthine libraries of the Holy Roman Vatican." He laughed menacingly, almost devilishly.

"No, no!" pleaded the Priest, "No, not my precious find, no, not the Vatican vaults!" he sobbed out, unabashedly, "not my dear Knights Templar. I've sought out that tome for years. Now it is mercilessly ripped from my feeble grasp." He looked up at the dirty boards overhead. "God forgive them for they know not what they do."

Geeze I felt so bad for the old wrinkled soul. God knows what he wanted with the ancient decaying manuscript. Hidden treasures of the Dark Ages. Salvation for his soul. Military maneuvers for footmen on horseback. Lost Roman roads for crusaders to Damascus. What was it that he imagined he would glean from those foreign words? And yet, I pitied his loss.

"You unworthy minister!" the Suit reprimanded, "ponder the effects of your vain and ridiculous life! May God strike you down for your foul and blasphemous leanings." He said it with so much feeling he was literally spitting the words at us. At that moment it seems something did strike down, and sure enough it did engage with the human flesh, for an extraordinarily large tome from a toppermost shelf plunged downward, meeting the bald head of the chastising Suit. There they lay upon the ground, the grim Suit and the book. An unabridged Bible with dubious Apocrypha (and all those extra pages and quotes King James censored out). It seems God had spoken.

We all just stood there for a minute and stared at each other. At this point in the book of my life, I'd become particularly antsy. I mean, let's get on with it. Was I to see Apricot again? Somehow I knew it must be so, I mean here I was living out my own memoirs, sure enough I would get what I wanted. And when would I see again my dear California? A haunting refrain of "California, Here I Come" seemed to subliminally whistle through the air. And I mighta heard the Almighty's voice, but I hadn't actually met Him and that seemed downright wrong. I mean it was His idea for me to be crowned this, this title of Messiah. I certainly wouldn't have chosen it for a career move. And what the hell did this Pope want? I was fed up!

"Let's get on with it. If I'm to meet this Pope, then let's get to it. I've had it with New York, I've had it with the media siege, and I've had it with this Princess of God stuff. Let's go!"

They grumbled amongst themselves for a moment, then off we went out the door (a Suit paid for the Templars book, it cost $49.95, and they wouldn't give him a break). Even though I had my hands tied behind my back and was flanked to either side by Suits, I marched boldly between the parting throngs. My head held high. The crowd was cheering me on. Some people were yelling, "Rock on, Michelle Domingue!" Someone draped me in a gauzy white robe, someone else put a wreathed contraption upon my head. Ken was at my side, smiling broadly.

"Geeze, Michelle, that's so great, you finally got your thorny crown. This is so perfect! The media will go crazy. We couldn't have planned it better. I mean, the handcuffs, the roaring crowds. Christ, Michelle, it's like the Macy's Parade!"

Indeed my temper was slowly ballooning. I was trudging quickly now through the parting Red Sea of peoples. The Suits could barely keep up. They had to trot and skip a bit every few steps, huffing and puffing, they were out of shape. I needed answers, and perhaps the Pope could help. If he wasn't willing, I'd strangle them out of him. Maybe this whole redeemer thing was the Pope's fault in the first place. Wasn't it the Pope that brought Christianity to a fevered pitch after Jesus? That's right. Jesus was just another Zionist crackpot rebel parading around the holy lands, hanging out with the Qumran priests spouting off his own religious and secular beliefs. Jesus was just one of a coupla hundred wacks running around proselytizing to a disgruntled countryside. Oh, he was popular all right. But it's the dying act that really brought down the house. Time and again it works. Elvis, Jim Morrison, Julius Caesar, Saint Joan—the people like a good death, and my stepbrother had an exceptional one. So along come these Christians, and one of them calls himself King Christian, er Pope, and says, yes um yes, this rebel is the one we shall call our Savior. That's not discounting my stepbrother's particular kind of charisma. There's no doubt the guy was a superstar of a zealot, all those fans hanging out with him day and night like he was Jerry Garcia. Free food from the admirers, women smoothing and pouring ointments, good wine, stealing horses for God. Jesus had a great act. I admire him a good deal.

But Jesus's act wasn't mine. I, Michelle Domingue, was to have a different and unique story, for I was the daughter of God and not the son.

Something was beginning to nag at me, a question. Who the heck were these twelve well-suited men and why were they acting for the Pope, and were they acting for the Pope? I halted them in the midst of our midtown march and posed the conundrum to the stern-faced twelve.

"By the way, sirs, who are you and why do I have my hands tied? This is certainly not the thirteen hundreds, and we do allow freedom of speech and thought in this here country of the United States of America."

The crowd burst out into a spontaneous "God Bless America." The twelve guys all looked at one another as though searching out an answer. "Well, well," stumbled one of them, "if you want we could take those cuffs off, ma'am. Would that help?"

"It most certainly would," I insisted, "who are you men, anyway?"

"Uh, another one mumbled, "well, to be honest..."

"Speak up my man, we can't hear you," I snapped. Why hadn't I asked this question before? I looked at the huge unending circle of faces about us. They were as puzzled as I. Everything quieted down till you could hear the mumbling Suit cough and clear his throat.

"Ma'am, we're actors and we got hired to come and get you and make a fuss and everything, 'cause they wanted to get it all on the TV and..."

"Oh damn," burst in Ken. He pushed his way past a coupla Suits, bounding to my side. "Damn it, Michelle, you're wrecking it, come on now, let's just march on."

"Ken, what on earth are you talking about? This whole thing is just a big bogus act? These guys here in suits aren't CIA/FBI or Pope soldiers, they're hired actors?"

"Quiet down now, Michelle, you see..." he was trying to whisper to keep the information from the thousands of hungry ears. "You see it would look so much better to meet the Pope like this. You know, with a little pizazz rather than, you know, just boom boom walk up, hello, shake hands, boom boom walk away, the end."

"Well," I wondered aloud, "Who in the world paid for this?"

"Um, the Apostles Assoc. for Michelle Domingue paid for it. But not these extras," he pointed to the vast throng. "They came on their own."

The crowd was as stunned as I. Someone stepped forward from the faceless many and offered me a life-sized cardboard cross. Someone else gave my patent leathers a quick spit shine.

"We still love and believe in you, Michelle Domingue," the cross-bearer said so gently, "please accept this humble gift."

Whew, I coulda clobbered Ken right there, but then the kindness of these gentle souls and the fake wooden cross put it all back into perspective. People were OK really. The twelve suited guys were taking off ties, coats and wingtips, turning back into the regular guys they truly were. One of them approached me. "I'm a real fan of yours, Michelle, would you mind signing the bottom of my wingtip? Sign it to Jim and Lonnie. My wife has all the books about you. Steve here," he pointed to an ex-Suit now regular guy actor, "Steve and I were kinda scared to meet you, we're such big admirers. Sorry if we spooked you back there at the bookstore. I usually get hired to play bad guys on TV."

Indeed he had the right bone structure for such a part.

"Well, Ken," I breathed out, "am I really to meet the Pope?"

"Oh that part is real, oh yeah. Don't worry, we called off the scaffold guys and the stake-and-bon-fire set. I just sent someone over there to tear it down, I promise no more pretend. But yeah, the Pope really is waiting for you."

"Well, Ken, you have shown yourself to be capable of much initiative and that is admirable. However, your creativity and plotline are sorely lacking. These are *my* memoirs, the life of me, Michelle Domingue, so let us walk forward into the truth, let us keep our eyes open and be not betrayed by myth, let us open our mouths only to utter realisms, that which we know to be true. Let us not tarry now but step forward to meet our future."

I got a firm grip on the cardboard cross and took a big step. The multitudes cheered as we walked on, releasing our past foibles, our misdeeds, our mistakes. We walked that day for each and and every spectator crunched in and crowded, unable to move themselves.

In due time we found our way through the legions of admirers. A galaxy of faces and arms seemed to gently reach out and touch me in my passing. By the time we reached the UN building, my once white gauze vestment was smudged and soiled, almost entirely brown. The thorny crown had been snatched by someone as a memento and in its place another follower had placed a white veil. The veil too had become dirt-brown. Fortunately for me, these outer trappings had saved my own dainty dress from the mussy rigors of messiahdom. I pulled a compact from my purse and double-checked my makeup, redo a line here, wipe off a smudge there and freshen the lipstick. I couldn't have looked lovelier. I simply could not meet the great Catholic Law-Bearer in brown, it wasn't a good color for me, and so off went those thoughtful gauzy vestures. After the blandness of the robe, my dress's unveiling seemed to brighten my outlook, and its perfect fit and sharp taste to dazzle the onlookers. I felt to be full of my womanness, and sure enough so many days had passed since the meager beginnings of my messiahdom, I surely had arrived at my full female potentiality. And I realized yes, it was time, I was starting my period.

The Pope was waiting for us. As we were approaching, I saw him checking his watch anxiously; then he looked up and saw us coming toward him. Ken was right, this was a real Pope, not a fake. He was in long white garb untouched by grubby human hand. His attire was so starch-white and wrinkleless, it appeared that he had been dressed instantly, an immaculate laundry miracle. We met and shook hands. The Pope was an old guy and didn't speak English. Fortunately, Priesty was with us, and they shook hands and blurbled in some foreign language. There were a bunch of robed characters with the Pope. Some of his sidekicks. They were looking me over real good. It was obvious that I was the best-dressed holy woman they'd ever seen.

They were introduced as Cardinal this and Archbishop that, a monk or two, and an abbot from some faraway monastery. Nobody spoke the same language, so we stood around and stared at each other. No matter what we did, the crowd seemed to like it, so we moved our mouths a bit as though saying something of significance. Then we waved at the crowd again and shook one another's hands. It was about this time that I became intensely aware of something. My flow had begun, and I had no female protective needs on hand. With my dainty dress and all these men in white robes, we could have a real problem, and so as a woman need do in a situation such as this, I spoke up.

"Listen I need someone to run over to a store and fetch me some super-maxis. Could someone do this, right away?" Priesty translated my plea to the Pope, who translated it to the Cardinal, who told it to the Archbishop. Things always end up being a big bureaucratic process when you deal with big cheeses. Finally a monk was instructed—he dashed to a nearby bodega. Back in a flash, the monk was a great runner, coming through the crowd at a good clip. He threw the box with one mighty pass. Ken caught it, made a quick jagged right past a blockade of crowd, and threw the box long into my arms. It was a well-thought-out and economical maneuver. I had the maxis now. I pumped my legs hard. There was nothing between me and the UN building. I was home free, touchdown!

I made it to the ladies' room just in the nick of time. Seems typical of a monk, he'd bought me the old-fashioned non-stickum pads, and one of those elastic one-size-fits-all belts. I couldn't blame him. He'd probably been holed up in some high stony cliff monastery overlooking the whole of the world for years. How could he have known what progress had been made in the last 30 years towards women's menstrual comfort? And yet, the belt and pad would do just fine. I was fitted now, and like all those commercials say, I could walk out into the world with a sense of confidence. I marched from the UN restrooms back out to my place amongst the Western world's leading holy men, with long feminist strides. My skirt excitedly swished from side to side, my arms swung back and forth self-assuredly, my hair bounced, seesawed, from side to side. I was a Charlie Girl, *Cosmopolitan* cover gal, Virginia Slims woman. I was all that of the past, and more. For I, Michelle Domingue, lived on the pinprick of the future/past, the match strike of the Now.

Though the Pope and his people seemed perfectly pleased with our mock exchange of mumbles some minutes ago, I, Michelle Domingue, was not. I intended to have a real conversation. Besides, I had so many questions for his boss, God. Somehow we would converse. No foreign language could impede my true mission. The Pope, his Pope friends and my friends were standing around staring at the mass of peoples. The peoples stared back. There were wooden blockades up now to hinder the throngs, to keep them from touching the Pope's garb, soiling it as mine had been dirtied. Nobody seemed to be saying anything, the holy men just stared out at the sea of faces, waving when the spirit struck. It was a lot like an eighth grade dance. The girls and boys didn't know how to mix it up. Everyone stood around not knowing what to do, looking stupid. I broke through the stupidity with a perfunctory Pope question.

"Sir, somehow I need to speak with you. Here is fine, I don't mind talking in front of the flocks."

He nodded, perhaps he understood.

"Sir Pope, I have somehow been chosen by the peoples of the world to live the life of a healer. A messiah, some say. Now, that's all very fine and dandy, however I still have not met in person God His/Herself. I find this rather alarming. It's like being hired as a major executive for a company where nobody has met the owner. In fact, it sounds a bit like L. Ron Hubbard's Scientology. I believe that I have heard the great divine Voice on at least one occasion. It seemed nice enough, and urged me to go about my savior work..."

My good Priesty cut in about here.

"Well, Michelle, that coulda been me, ya know, if it was back at the Salty Lion. But..."

"You see, Pope sir, that means I've probably never even heard the Lord Cosmo's voice. You see, and what right do I have then to be a messiah? Yes, you nod at me, but what about you, what right have you or this cardinal? And yet you give out laws and goin'-to-Hells like you're on first name terms with the Grand One. I mean, excuse me for being outspoken, but I am a woman and I'm on my period, and therefore I can say whatever I want."

The Pope mumbled under his breath and nodded affirmatively.

"Now sir, one thing I don't get is how any religion, yours or others, can say they are the truest word of God? That God would be happier if we all just religioned in one way? But that doesn't quite make sense. All the animals are so different, the plants, even molecules, are quite different. It would be pretty miserable if there was only one force of nature, and that was, say, gravity. We'd all be a bunch o' pancakes. You don't have to answer now.

"Between the two of us, maybe we could appeal to the Big Creator right here right now, in front of these people and the flying flags of the UN and the TV eyeball of the world. Maybe we could just ask God, whether He, She or It, to come on down now, pop by for a few minutes of Q and A. No pressure. Just like to get a glimpse. What does the Master of the Universe look like? How did you get all that stuff into the primeval atom that exploded into the creation of all present matter? Why do some women have miserable menstrual periods, and others a faint gesture of feminine corporeality?"

The Pope nodded, and then, with an in-sightful twinkle in his eye, winked at me. The Pope was affirming my request for God's immediate presence.

"God come down to us!" I hollered, and the avenues of people let out a tremendous yelp. Everyone became very excited, and murmured betwixt themselves. My dear priest friend edged toward me. He had ahold of the lifelike cardboard crucifix, but was looking rather nervous. His eyes were shifting from side to side, as though he were awaiting an invisible opponent.

"Michelle, Michelle Domingue, in all due respect I do not think this a show of wisdom, this yelling, lest the Holy of Holies come flying down, raining upon us like pounding pumice from a froth-ing firmament."

"Well, dear Priesty one, how then would you have me call upon the Majestic Cloud?"

"Perhaps you could just wait it out in hermetical silence, say within the solitude of a high elevation cave or even the knee-bending tranquility of the foot of your bed."

"So you're saying God doesn't like loudness. I don't think this is true, kindly Priest. I, Michelle Domingue, will dredge up the spontaneous words that have thus far served me so well. I will stand by my God-given talents. And like a good parent, my Father will come to me, pat me on the shoulder, and say, 'Well done, my Michelle, let me take it to work tomorrow, and I will Xerox your verbal expressions for the good of all.' And then He will correct my misspellings, and make us all a cup of cocoa. Yes cocoa for all."

A great hurrah rang out from the throaty horde. God simply couldn't let me down now. Here I was in front of the Pope, New York, Ken's friends, and who knows how many office fax machines. God would come through. I took a deep fulfilling breath, and put my faith in something none of us could see. The streets went quiet. All that could be heard was the deep heaving sighs of me, Michelle Domingue. The windy refrain spiralled and spun uncontrollably down the quiet city corridors. Breathing got me to thinking, gave me pause for reflection, and so in thinking I thought and in thought I did think. And a great outpouring of celluloid did reel through my movie projector, and I sat in the cinema house alone watching the frames flicker by. A delicate tune ferried through, something simple and stirring for piano and guitar. A repeating refrain, back and forth it went, a soulful redundancy. Off it would go a note or two, then back to reiteration of a theme that brought my heart up, up to my throat, to my nose, burning my sinuses, up further still to my eyes, my eyes. An unending sounding. A repetend. The breathing, the breathing.

And then the rumble began. The low dog note rolled, seismographed through my serene daydream. It Tyrannosaurus-Rexed my sweet herbivorous lament. It brought me back to the crowds, the Pope, the Big Hoohah. What was this damnable grumble of sound? It was a large vehicle approaching us personages at the forefront of the multitudes, moving through the barricades and bumping up onto the UN lawn, coming closer. It was one of those puke-green buses with small barred windows that sit at the side of the road and you always think: "they're transporting a whole pack of criminals from one prison to another." Only it's not the hardened law-breakers you thought they were, just a bunch of trash-pickers who got a moving traffic violation that went unpaid. Well here they were pulled up right next to me, Michelle Domingue, the Pope and the Holy Faces.

The Pope was trying to get my attention, so was the dear Priestly. They were both poking me with their pointy hard fingers, waving hands in front of my face. I had been so transfixed by my own thought journey and then the jolting tones of the bus growl, I had not even seen what was before my very eyes, hadn't recognized the human touch. I suspect now that I had gone into a deep state of samadhi, or a place of communion with the huge Unspeakable One. God, I know now, spoke to me in a deep reverent silence and then, in silence, taught me another language, the God language, which he conveyed to me by musical movements and cinematic hieroglyphs. I felt completely satisfied that my prayer had been heard, my screech to God acknowledged, answered. I could face the faceless throngs now knowing that I was the real McCoy, a person for the people, a truth in the wake of forgery.

The Pope was jabbering about something in his foreign language. None of us had any idea what he was saying. Everyone in the crowd watched his jaw move up and down, his hands gesticulate to accompany vocal inflection, his white dress blow prettily in the breeze. Then, like an exceptionally slow tennis match, our heads typewriter-carriaged over to the translator, Priestly.

"Michelle Domingue, the Pope would like to pay his respects to your greatness of spirit by giving you a gift. He says it's very ordinary to give titles and certificates of say, honorary priest or Saint. Instead, he would like to give you something that comes from the heart of the Vatican."

The monk handed a thing to the archbishop who gave it to the cardinal who gave it to the Pope, and then, at last, the Pope turned to me, Michelle Domingue. The thing was not unlike the paper crucifix that Ken was now playing with on the lawn (laying it out on the grass, Ken posed himself over the cross like Jesus, and was pretending to be in the throes of the Holy Death, trying out different positions). The gift was a good-sized piece of cardboard in the shape of a key. Gold glitter had been sprinkled and glued to the whole thing, I guess to make it look like a real key. Then there were little pictures pasted over the glitter, Polaroids of sacred material objects.

The Shroud of Turin, a closeup of a skull with a caption that read "Pope Urban I," a picture of a cup that looked like the Holy Grail, a piece of an old wooden stake with red smears, one leather sandal, a decomposing and out-of-date maternity bra, and a bunch of other photos too. Looked like someone threw it together at the last minute. I could still smell the Bluebird brand glue.

The Pope was doing his mumbling thing and then our heads again shot back to Priestly.

"Michelle Domingue, here is the greatest gift the Church could ever give you. A big fake key that symbolizes the key to the Vatican vaults."

"But dear Priestly, tell the Pope thank you, but why did he go to all the trouble of making this phony key when it wouldn't unlock even a car door? Tell the Pope I would like the real key, and thank you, but I have no place to put this curious pasteboard souvenir."

After the two of them communicated, the Pope nodded at me, and then, unhooking his collar from the back, reached his hand awkwardly down past his collarbone, fished for something, then out came his hand with a little gold glint on a fine silver chain. Here was the true key to the Catholic mysteries. I, Michelle Domingue, took it (that key to the Holiest of Materialisms) and placed it gingerly about my neck. The Pope broke his stoicism and smiled. I smiled back. All was good and the crowd cheered on.

Chapter Ten

Ken had stopped playing with the bogus crucifix and dashed over to me, he was in one of his excited but gagged states. He was jumping up and down, pointing somewhere, generally acting as though in a state of seizure. And though the Pope and his people were alarmed, we knew our dear Ken well enough to surmise he had some little something to communicate to us. The Priest grabbed him, held him down. and I gave him a simple but effective punch in the diaphragm. A globule of words came vomiting out, not unlike the fabulous throat singers of Tuva. Ken pulled out a hanky, wiped his face and the back of his neck, took in a deep breath and spoke articulately.

"Whew. Well done, my dear friends. Michelle Domingue, you are the first to move me past that childhood speech impediment. I graciously thank you."

"You're very welcome, my dear Ken. But what was it you were in such a hurry to tell?"

"Well, Michelle..."

Barely had the words sprung from his lips when I caught sight of...

"Apricot, Mr. Apricot. I believe he's over there with that, sort of chain gang, the state-funded bus."

I saw him, I did, I saw Apricot. An irresistible force had caught hold of me, and I was unable to move. My eyes were all that worked. There he was, the long lost once-upon-a-time love, Mr. Apricot. He looked good too. There he was by the pale green bus, easy to spot, he and his yoke-mates wore bright orange reflector vests and matching construction hats. There's nothing like a man in a uniform. His sleeves were rolled up, an old work shirt, and I could see the muscles in his arms bulging and moving, as he fiercely lanced at a fleck of trash, pierced it through then scooped it into his orange bag of bounty.

A swooning quartet of emotions swelled up from my heart chakra as I saw him workedly bagging our discarded waste. Paper cups, pizza plates, cigarette butts, confetti, paper banners blown in from the crowd that said things like "Michelle Domingue + the Pope = LOVE," "Michelle Domingue for President," etc. etc. Even the glue and glitter key to the Vatican and the paper crucifix, all manner of waste. Unwanted orphaned objects, obsolete baggage harvested from living trees, animals and plastic to make a nice moment as a paper decoration and then banished. "Siberia!" Apricot, there he was, hovering amongst the unwanted. He had a two-day-old beard, his glasses were bent, he was dejectedly hunched at the shoulders, and yet in him was the course of the Everyman. In him was this working class hero, the ol riches-to-rags tale. It's remarkable that we even recognized him amongst the nine or ten other foundlings, all in orange vests and hats. (The fallen wear the same ill-fitting garb.) I couldn't stop staring. And then I wondered, what in heaven's name had happened to Apricot, that once strapping ambitious manager of Neiman-Marcus, that intellectual giant in the world of physics, that good honest husband with a wife on Long Island? ("Oh my, how far the angel's fallen, the train's gone off the track.") And so too I wondered what had ended the reign of the mighty reptiles? If the long-suffering/surviving dinosaurs couldn't carry on, what chance have we, humankind? When the Earth's tilt moves just so and the temperature goes just to the left or right might we too die out in mass, us large mammalia, high on the food chain? And like those monstrous animals of old, my beloved Apricot had met his own Cretaceous period.

He was hunkered over bagging a large clump of garbage, and then he looked up. I knew somehow my staring at him would finally blaze through that hard-hat of his and strike a love chord of familiarity. Apricot and I locked eyes and it was Valentine's Day in the middle of autumn. I flushed red then white, then blue, I wasn't breathing. I took a breath. The involuntary functions were all off whack.. Breathe in, breathe out. I wanted to run to him, grab him and smash him to me, and in my mind I did and my mental dress became mussed from his sexy orange uniform. Orange orange! Apricots are orange. He smelled like garbage but I suddenly loved garbage, it was my favorite perfume. I wanted to pull him down into the heaped orange bags of trash and roll around in the decadence of our manifested desire. And yet I did not do such a thing, I only looked and thought.

And then I noticed, where was his ring? An impulse overtook me that my mind had little to do with. Suddenly my legs were moving, I was running, I was running towards Apricot. Priestly and Ken were calling after me, the crowd began to ooh and ahh. The Pope and his cronies mumbled their jumbled utterances. I simply didn't know what I was doing. Perhaps in retrospect I was acting rashly. Although it was, I do know now, not myself that moved me that day but a greater force. The omniscient and original ACT. I felt myself dashing, charging at full speed, and at first I thought, yes, maybe my womanly wiles are taking me back to the ladies' powder room, and then that other part of me said, "no, Michelle Domingue, you need not visit the little girls' room yet. You need to run thisaway." And so like a finely tuned torpedo, I wobbled and corrected my course, while the whole of the city looked on. And then I saw my target, my feets were taking

172

me straight for a collision with Apricot. He saw me coming, and just yards before our colliding he darted a quick left. My feet caught on quick, and before I could think a thought I was moving for him. I chased him cross the whole of the UN lawn. He was a good four lengths ahead of me. But my feets had no worries. We ran back and forth across that lawn a good four times before Ape decided to go a new route, out into the multitude of onlookers. You'd think my feets would lose him amongst all those other shuffling shoes, and yet they did not. I was on his tail. Now and again a breeze would puff down the avenue, catch a few of Apricot's molecules and blow them in the direction of my nostrils. It did smell of springtime, though I knew it to be deep fall. It did remind me of my teenaged youth, it did remind me of my father's pool, of my initial gaze into the eyes of the Apricot. It did conjure up my initial vision and the dramatic bump on the head, it was Prunus Armeniaca, a precocious blossoming. And I was ready to pick the fruit.

Yes, my mind was catching up with what my body was doing. The feet had it first, then the legs, then a great vibrating rumble from my root chakra. I had thought that I had needed a restroom but no, it was simply the quaking of my lower continental plates rubbing one against the other. My stomach had butterflies — the tummy worms had metamorphosed. My heart lit up, skipped a beat, did a jump kick shuffle-off-to-Buffalo, and my throat choked and did its darnedest to hold back the troops. The enemy was storming the fortress! Scaling the walls "like thick swarms of locusts" finally to break through and wrench itself upstream like hopping salmon to the toppermost platform, the mind of me, Michelle Domingue. And then I knew I was chasing Apricot for good reason.

Oh dear readers, when someone has betrayed a beloved there is no mercy upon his wretched, pitiless soul. There is no place in heaven for a thief that has stolen away a pure untainted heart. For even if the love organ is found and returned to its rightful owner, it alas has been tarnished, never to return to its original state of innocence again. Even a joyride upon the heart of another does not go unnoticed. For the secret recesses of the breast are looking, listening, always thinking. Like a very small child, helpless, watching from its cradle.

And so I long jumped, I needed to make up for the two lengths between me and Mr. Apricot. If my running couldn't make-up the gap, my jumping could. I'd been a darn good long jumper in Junior High, and had even gone on to place fourth in the country's Junior Olympics, probably my single-most trophitic possibility. My father had such high-reaching hopes, and then in a snap-of-a-twig moment they were dashed beyond repair, for fourth-place winners are losers, and a trophy was not given me that sunny sad day. Nonetheless I knew my jumpin' legs still to be good, and in this chase of an instance they could heed me well. I jumped, leapt into the air with a force unknown to me before. I leapt with a strength unequaled. And pounced then upon the well-formed if shocked frame of sweet Mr. Apricot. Within seconds I had him stretched out upon the asphalt of the avenue. The tremendous crowd created a crater of a circle around us, watching intently, wondering what I, Michelle Domingue, would do to this man, this *National Enquirer* of a life, this Brutus. And at that very moment, I wondered as well.

"Michelle Domingue must you always grab and pin me? I haven't even said word one to you, and there you go chasing me around the UN making me a fool for the world to see..."

"Perhaps, dear Apricot, once a fool always a fool. You got a whole lotta explainin' to do. What do you say for yourself?"

"I know what you're thinkin', Mich, you're thinkin', aren't I ashamed of myself? Well, goldarnit, I'm not...could you please remove your point of an elbow from my ear? Thank you. I'm not ashamed of what I've done, I'm a red-blooded American male, and if you were one you'da done the same thing. Besides, what kinda manager do you think I was after your arrival?—everyone comin' up to me: 'Say, sir, where are the alligator shoes? oh my you're that famous Mr. Boyfriend of Michelle Domingue.'

I couldn't stand it, Mich, I really fuckin' hated that. And then the whole department store of people gathering around me, me a simple store manager, and asking for miracles, like: materialize a size twelve blue floral pattern in such and such a line, or the elevator light's out , turn it back on, or make my credit card readout approved. Bullshit stuff! All the integrity of being an anonymous merchant of a long line of merchants dating back to the camel caravans of Phoenicia. All that out the window, destroyed by the arrival of you 'messiah' you, Michelle. Damn it."

He had a touching construct of a story, even the crowd and the TV news crews looked at one another and mumbled betwixt themselves.

"You plead a very good case, Mr. Apricot, and yet there is in the thick of your plight a great missing quotient..."

I said it, but I didn't quite know what I was getting at. Maybe somehow in the saying it would unravel its ball of twine, its shrouded mystery. I kept him tightly between me and the pavement while I thought it over.

Now, sometimes in our lives when a great conundrum is pressed upon us and we, like the human animals we are, look on dumbly with mouth agape, there flies in a buzz of an insect. The bum was that fly. He came to us ascending from the stinking dank of a disrepaired subway staircase, and proceeded

176

towards our inner circle with a crowd-moving odorous aplomb. He was a caveman of a being. An abominable brown man.

Far off in the distance was the crackling sound of a public address system. Vaguely I heard my name beseeched, a faint-sounding call that could have been man or mind. These yearning cries I did not heed, for I had the heartbeat of my Apricot beneath me, and the mesmerizing magnetism of the clearly approaching bum. All heads did turn. And something different than my period did shudder in my womb. One of the darnedest things about that very timely bum was his unbroken brownness. He seemed to be caked in a fine brown silt that covered hair and hide. Hair covered head and face, and out of the bald spot peered two lines for eyes, two slits that peered out strikingly, darting hither and which way, shining brightly like the very sun. Something brand new shone out mysteriously, from that hurricane of decay.

I loosened my grasp of Apricot, my fingers unlocked from the pinch of skin. He could finally move to twist his head toward me and, seeing my beguiled expression, swiveled his head in the direction of my gaze.

"Dear me," he mewed.

All eyes had moved from me, Michelle Domingue, to the OTHER, the bum, and the bum was inching my way.

Then finally he did arrive at my now sitting-up side, seeing almost nothing now but the large eclipse of a man, striking all from view but he. He grumbled pathetically and somehow sympathetically to me. I couldn't tell you, dear readers, what language it was he did speak, and yet it was most enigmatically a tongue I did understand all too well. Clusters of sputters, guttural grunts, hand gestures and Oghamian nose scratches. All signals, odd inscriptions for communication purposes. Sometimes he would keyboard on his shinbone a string of words for my hearing alone. The crowd, thinking it to be a betrancing form of blues music, hushed and fell into an enchanted fog.

This is what he said:

"I have seen them coming and they will arrive soon, so my words with you my Lordess will be brief. They approach in a cloud of rumble upon the Earth, and they bring with them a rolling thing. So only now for this brief instant do I have the privilege of time. Let loose your disagreements with the Prince at your side, and see him as thus."

And then he did scratch a rock upon the paved ground. A faint set of letters appeared. They made a square as thus:

```
A   O   U   E   I
O               E
U               U
E               O
I   E   U   O   A
```

And then a series of letters which changed places, and made no sense till the bum explained them with nose scratches. Those letters read:

A
P
R
I
C
O
T

Of course now it was recognizable as my dear Mr. Apricot's fruiticious surname. But what besides love made his name so, well, mentionable? The bum rescrambled the letters to: ACT PRIO or ACT PRIOR. He shook his head up and down enthusiastically.

"Yes Michelle, the Prior Act. What was the Act before the origin of origins? The answer lies mysteriously in the letters of Apricot's name. The answer is "Armeniaca. Prunus. Roe. Yew. Quince. Omega. Tetragrammaton. Yes, you see, the Alpha, the birth of birth, the youth, the accomplishment. The death and resurrection. All in the scope of a name. Apricot."

So what then did that all mean, that Ape was the messiah and I was not? That Ape had a fanciful tag? That, perhaps, Ape was the Jesus to my, well, my Michelle Domingue? Had God gotten Messiah Domingue and Messiah Jesus together at last?

It is likely the answer lies veiled within the letters of his name, Prunus Armeniaca, Apricot. And what was his other name? Scarcely have I mentioned it within the pages of this book, and yet it was his other name that first brought him to me, the other name that perhaps was once held dear to the hearts of camel-driving merchants of Sumeria. The other name, Joshua. For strangely enough, his name was Joshua Apricot Isaacs.

I now looked away from the eye-sparkling brown bum, and gazed upon the sheer clean human beauty of dear Apricot. Oh, the mystery, all the mystery he was to me hung in the air, and in the sound of his fabulous name, "Apricot."

The ground-moving rumble was approaching as the deep earth-oozing bum had predicted. Within no time he had somehow vanished into the thick of the populace, no doubt to seek out another entrance to his deep cavernous existence. An alternate chasm into the gaping depths.

I looked at Apricot and he looked at me. Somehow our differences had grown wings and flown away. Our index fingers touched. It felt like the silk of a flower. My eyes got a little fuzzy, and it made Ape look like a well-touched-up photo for a high class girlie mag. Or the porcelain skin and dewy eyes that peer out at you from a David Hamilton book.

"I want to have sex with you, Ape," I innocently confessed. And with the word 'confession' came the thought of the Pope and my dear Priestly. Geeze, where were they now?

"Yes yes, Michelle, and I want to have sex with you, but these multitudes of people and..."

"And of course," I wanted to know the truth now, "you are married, my beloved."

"Oh that, well. You could call it marriage, but not tomorrow. We filed for divorce just yesterday. I'm afraid, my dearest, I did fail at staying away from you. For I pined away for three days and three nights. Needless to say, I could take it no more and fell into the depths of despair. Yes, Michelle, I piled sin upon sin. I drank and gambled, smoked and caroused. I was a hollow shell of a man. Now I'm working off my debt to society by cleaning roadsides and parks for the city. I thought there was no hope for me, till I saw your loveliness once again and, well, I realize that I fucked up in leaving and all that..."

Ah, all the words I had wished for, had given up hope for. Here they were, and the taste was sweet. It was then and there, in front of all, that we we leaned toward one another for a kiss that would seal our reconciliation and open the sexual floodgates.

But something kept our lips from connecting, a very large vibration now intruded upon our dreamy bubble. It was the arrival of the bum's Prediction. The rumble was here. Yes, the rumble was here, and so too a battalion of horse-riding men draped in white with bold red crosses upon their breasts. Here too were the Pope and his robed buddies, the podium and public address system having been squeaky-wheeled down the street. Here too were my dear friends Ken Jackowitz and Priestly. It was a big party, with the big event shrouded in God knows how many yards of cloth. Yes, the rolling rumble had arrived, come to us through the parting sea of people, a veiled thing some 30 feet tall on a wooden dolly. The crusader horsemen stopped, and did a fancy maneuver in unison with their swords. Ken dashed over to my side.

"That's the Freemasons, Michelle, this is a big hoopla and they're honoring you by dressing as crusaders. Cool, eh?"

"Hmm," I offered. Whatever they were doing they were interrupting, for I had it in my mind now that I was ready to consummate my re-found love for Apricot. I'd had it with all this spiritual religious mystic gubble, and was ready to let a cigar be a cigar. And what a cigar my dear Apricot did brandish.

Priestly did interrupt my Earthly desires.

"Michelle Domingue, I'm sorry to say the Pope would like to have his key to the Vatican back. He says he made a frightful mistake and," he then whispered: "frankly Michelle, between you and me, if he's given it to you take it, take it and run. Take it and open the vaults for the whole world to see, to scrutinize, to fondle."

Well I wasn't going to give it back and I wasn't going to run. No, not just yet, for even if Apricot and I had a date with delicious decadency, I had this one card remaining, this one card still to be played out on God's gamblin' table.

The Masonic horsemen blew some trumpets and bumped a drum. Someone crackled out a word or two over the PA, "Blah Blah Michelle Domingue," and then Boom! down came the veil, down fell the coverlet from the Trojan-Horsed THING.

It was me! It was me and then I pinched myself, it wasn't me because I was here pinching myself. But in essence it was me, an extremely large rendering of me, Michelle Domingue. It wasn't that I was so surprised to see a statue of myself (for I'd come to accept all forms of adulation). It was simply eye-ogling to see a 30-foot-high head. The head of Michelle Domingue. The crowd was hushed for a moment, then they all cried, "Speech, speech!"

I looked at Apricot, and then timidly took my place behind the podium. The Pope and the Archbishop got behind me and began fingering my neck, groping through my pockets, hunting for the Vatican key. It felt quite good, I surely was in need of a deep massage, and this laying on of hands was the remedy. I relaxed immediately.

"Thank you, thank you. Truly I'm honored by this very large marble Head. I must say the hair is coifed in a most pleasing manner."

"Give us a great insight," interrupted someone, a blessed follower, and the rest of the tireless throng chimed in.

"Give us, give us," they repeated in unison.

But at the moment I was preoccupied with something that was giving it to me. Sure, the fondling massage I was receiving from the holy men was helpful, but still my body was wrenching in painful contorts. Since my one trip to the little girls' room I hadn't returned. Now my body was making a convincing, undeniable case. The damnable cramps had begun. Oh geeze, if only I could get ahold of some aspirin (ibuprofen). I buckled over, oh the wretched pain I felt that grand day.

"I...I need an aspirin," I managed to get out. And so, God knows how many pills were thrown our direction. A shower of over-the-counter and pre-scribed tablets snowed upon us. It was a lovely sight, like the first fallen white. I merely opened my mouth and let a few capsules fall in, gulped them down, and within minutes was able to stand tall again. With aspirin all men are created equal.

"Thank you so much, my flock. You see, where there was none, now there is an abundance. I believe the universe works in such ways. Now let me excuse myself, humbly, for I have to see to my feminine needs."

A very small child on a crutch stepped forward from the many and addressed me.

"Please, Ma'am, accept this modest offering."

Its dewy eyes looked sweetly upon me, and hands together it lifted the thoughtful gift. A stick-on super-maxi. A profoundly appropriate tribute. I gathered it thankfully. The screeching voice of a woman yanked the crippled child back into the arena of peoples.

"Get back here, you witch of a child!"

I'll never know who the woman was nor the child, but to this day each time I use a super-maxi, I say a silent prayer.

Chapter Eleven

If the huge Head of me, Michelle Domingue, was good for nothing else, it at least was a good pee bush. For the dark side of the marbled monstrosity created such utter sunlessness, I was able to do my feminine business in relaxed nonchalance, unviewed. I was clean now. Pure again. Chaste and white. Besides my period all I could think of was Apricot. Somehow I had to get at him, get away from the multitudinous peeping of eyes. I didn't even feel the umph to get back out in from of them all, I just wanted to snatch Ape from the podium, and pull him into this lovely cool darkness.

I leaned heavily upon the marble obelisk. Oh, what to do? And then it was that I did remember my meeting with the Rock and Buddha. Why, there could actually be an entity or more here in this stone, here at my fingertips! I listened in a deep indescribable manner. Perhaps the great stone Head could bail me outta this fix, find me and Apricot a way to make our love getaway.

Next thing I knew, my hands began to sink into the mineral. It felt like water, buoyant, but lighter, more like you'd imagine antigrav. It all went so very fast, suddenly I was talking to my stone Head while physically merged with it.

"Listen, Stone, I need some help."

"Yes, yes, Michelle Domingue, we of this marble face know of you through our interconnecting molecular communications. Our friend of the mesa told us of your visit. What could we of this stone do for you?"

"Well, if you could somehow keep a message for the people that visit you. Give them a good feeling, something they can hold onto. See, I don't have time to say a proper farewell here. My human biological clock is ticking, and I need my time with my man Apricot. Give the people a good feeling message."

"We would be happy to oblige. There is a little spot down by the sculpted lips that a human can sit near and we will create a good sensation for them. Leave that to us, Michelle Domingue."

"Thank you, Stone Head, you minerals are good beings."

And at that I was back in the Earthly reality I've come to recognize as home.

There was Ape next to Ken and Priestly. The Pope was boarding his Popemobile, waving goodbye like a Miss America winner. The crowd was roaring deafeningly. Many cries for Michelle Domingue were heard from the quake of sound. The people were restless, like animals frenzied at the water hole. My God, how would we ever get outta here alive? Then I remembered I had a rape whistle in my dainty purse. I used it at once. The shrillness bore a hole through the thick thunderous roar of voices. I waved at Ape from the dark side of the Head. My arm was visible only, but he knew its beauticious contours as mine alone.

I must say now, my dear readers, that I was not quite clear whether my work as a savior was to end that day, or whether it would take me into further saintly endeavors. I did know that there was a 5 PM Greyhound bus, destination USA, waiting for Ape and myself if we could get ourselves to Port Authority.

Ape took my hand, and the two of us ran crosstown like the dickens, ran together, ran with a like goal in mind, for the throngs were not far behind. Ken and Priestly were just behind us, and we could say our breathless goodbyes while we made good ground.

"Michelle Domingue, don't forget us at the AAMD. Fax in your whereabouts, get to us on the Net. We're your Mother's Little Helper. Stay in good with the news media. Remember those suggestions I made. Try the Pope having an affair with... We love you, Michelle Domingue."

And then my dear Priester:

"Thank you for being the Lamb, sacrificing your time, hearing my darkest secrets. You know, I think I'm on the straight and narrow now. I've even started a home for wayward and drug-riddled teens. You've given my old life hope again. Hallelujah, Elijah has come!"

And though the restless throngs tried to catch Apricot and me, Michelle Domingue, but for the grace of God they did not. No, not their flesh merely, their long-pass shouts. "We love you Michelle, oh Lamb of God!" "Behold, the messiah Michelle walks amongst us!" "You are of our blood, of our flesh, yet you are the divine manifest!" and etc. Counterpointing these ecstatic shouts of approval were the dissonant shouts of the Archbishop, the Cardinal and their furious henchmen.

"We will get that key if it means hunting you down to the ends of the Earth. Vengeance is ours!"

The damnable Vatican vaults. I didn't have the key now, anyway. I'd tossed it to its new owner. Someone who knew its worth, Priestly.

The rejoicing crowds were waving their good-byes from a half block behind.

Yes, I'd come to love and feel gentle comfort in the passionate admiration of the N.Y. flock, and yet there were others now to see. There were still those that knew only of my name through a photograph or an article in *Newsweek*, *Time*, the *Enquirer*. Apricot and I were boarding a Greyhound bus to find a time

190

and place for our love. Still, we both knew that my work was bigger than the both of us. There would be no running from the Messiah tag, but there could be moments away from it. Like the woman I became that day in the small of the bus urinal. The swaying and turning of the Greyhound bothered us none. We passengers were twisting our way outta the bowels of New York City, but Ape and I were traveling other realms, the realms of the man/woman touch. The Past begone! Here IS the moment!

Epilogue

It is here that I must leave you, faithful readers.
The memoirs of a life are a difficult task to
undertake. And my life has been a most peculiar
one. These here pages would not even be before you
had not the Grand Higher One impelled me to do
so. There is so much more of my life, so many people who have not made it into this binding, and then
there are the yous that I am still to meet. For it may
be so that I will one day Greyhound into *your* town.
But as of this writing I am making my way west, for
I have heard the calling, the daily movement of the
sun, the nightly rotation of the stars, their dramatic
dance across the black velvet stage. All to fall into
the cool blue of the Pacific. And it is to California I
go. The fatso autumn moon beckoning me. The
omniscient essence of grape vineyards. The seasonal
procession marches on, and winter creeps ever
closer. Somewhere now in California, a Mexican
laborer stoops before a single cotton flower and con-
templates its prickled beauty. A surfer swivels his

longboard round to face the melting cheddar cheese of sun. A young Angelino views with pride the rosy new tattoo on his girlfriend's thigh, kisses her brown hair and chucks a stone into the grey glass of Echo Park Lake. Just north of Eureka a camera-toting tourist stops at a roadside diner, buys an expensive piece of salmon jerky, unabashedly hugs the soft bark of an ancient sequoia and cries. And cries as I now do, vainly holding this implement of technology, this representation of my innermost thoughtly wanderings, a drooling of inky musings. This pen! Oh, this pen, carrying my message across the span of miles. A message perhaps one day to be found in a protective vault or clay urn unearthed by a race of terrestrial peoples our century flare of brain cannot conceive. Oh, you pen, guiding me these many days. Oh, technological breakthrough!, bringing together both feather and inkwell, instrument to be set aside, left now to those dear future days, in the hopes that their new, unheard voice will call upon your inky use. And will I, Michelle Domingue, exist without you? I'm afraid to lay you down. I sit here upon this vinyl seat, soft enough, that transports me now across the bulge of Earth called America, that takes me past the furthest mesa, west. And takes me through the infinite gold of October corn, takes me over the rushing red main veins, Mississippi, Missouri, Rio Grande, Colorado, hairpins me up and over and round the chocolate brown bumps, ear-popping ice cream peaks, golden eagle swayin', Indian prayin', canyons. And low-high flatland that holds stories of UFO hoverings and wigwam motor inns and saguaro-poachin' grammas passing us, heading west too in rickety windblown RVs.

Oh, where will I be without you, pen, without you, page? I will be in the grapes, the soft bark, the rippled reservoir water, the apricot trees and the lolling brown ball of harvest moon that languidly climbs above the dirty autumn breeze. To you followers whose fates and mine do not somehow intertwine, who do not find my *Newsweek* stories, who can't get ahold of *The New York Times*, who don't have a friend that did attend my famed appearances, and who nowhere can buy Apricot's *In and Out of Bed with Michelle Domingue*... Take heart. I'm almost always to be found in California.

Cindy Lee Berryhill is a singer-songwriter
who has recorded five albums. This is her
first novel.

CDs by Cindy Lee Berryhill:

Who's Gonna Save the World?
Naked Movie Star
Garage Orchestra
Straight Outta Marysville
Living Room 16

Printed in the United States
50512LVS00001B